Welcome Everypony

Fluttershy

Rainbow Dash

Twilight Sparkle

Spike

Welcome to this Essential Handbook, packed full of everything you need to know about **MY LITTLE PONY.**

Join the **Mane Six** as they take you on a tour of Equestria. Along the way you can follow their adventures from all nine seasons of *Friendship is Magic*, *MY LITTLE PONY: THE MOVIE*, and special episodes *Best Gift Ever* and *Rainbow Roadtrip*.

Then, get to know all the ponies' friends, with full fact files on everycreature and all their cutie marks.

Lets go!

Rainbow Dash's faithful pet, **Tank**, is being mischievous and has hidden himself on some of the pages in this guide. Can you find him? See where he's hidden on page 206.

Rarity

Pinkie Pie

Applejack

Map of Equestria

THE UNKNOWN

BUG
BEAR
TERRITORY

STARLIGHTS
CAVE

TROTTINGHAM

GRIFFONSTONE
STATION

GRIFFISH
ISLES

N

GUTO RIVER

GUTO

R

UNS

GRIFFONSTONE

CELESTIAL
SEA

BE
HERE

DRAGON'S LAIR

Equestria is home to lots of magical creatures, not just Ponies. Here are some of the creatures **Twilight Sparkle** can't wait for you to meet! Can you figure out where they live?

Pony
Earth, Pegasus, Unicorn and Alicorn

Zebra

Kirin

Dragon

Yak

Griffin

Changeling

Seapony

Friendship is Magic

Twilight Sparkle, Pinkie Pie, Rainbow Dash, Rarity, Applejack and Fluttershy are the Mane Six and the best of friends. When Twilight Sparkle is first sent to Ponyville by her mentor, Princess Celestia, she is not so sure about the ponies who live there. But after discovering the magic of friendship with these five ponies, Twilight Sparkle couldn't think of anywhere better to call home.

Before long, the six best friends go on adventures all over Equestria, from battling Nightmare Moon and reuniting her with her sister, to reforming the Spirit of Chaos and Disharmony, Discord. All these adventures earn Twilight the title of Princess of Friendship and the wings to match! She decides to set up the School of Friendship, so that everycreature has the chance to learn about the magic of friendship.

Where it all began

Once upon a time, in the magical land of Equestria, there were two sisters who ruled together and created harmony for all the land.

The elder sister, **Princess Celestia,** raised the sun at dawn and the younger, **Princess Luna,** brought out the moon to begin the night. Together, the sisters maintained a fair and balanced kingdom for all who lived there.

But as time passed, the younger princess grew jealous that ponies spent their days awake and slept through the beautiful nights she created. Then one day, **Princess Luna** refused to lower the moon at dawn, vowing to cast eternal night-time over Equestria. Her anger transformed her into a wicked mare, **Nightmare Moon,** and no amount of reasoning would stop her.

Princess Celestia had no choice but to use the strongest magical power she knew of – the Elements of Harmony. Using the magic of the Elements, **Princess Celestia** banished her sister to the moon, leaving her to rule over the kingdom by herself.

Season One

1

We meet **Twilight Sparkle,** a student at **Princess Celestia's** School for Gifted Unicorns. **Twilight** loves studying but isn't very good at making friends, so **Celestia** sends her to Ponyville, with her assistant **Spike,** to meet new ponies.

Did you know?

Twilight recruits **Owlowicious** as a new pet to help her study through the night.

2

Twilight soon meets **Pinkie Pie, Rainbow Dash, Rarity, Fluttershy** and **Applejack.** They welcome her to Ponyville, but **Twilight** is not sure why she needs friends – surely books can teach her everything?

3

But when **Princess Celestia** is kidnapped before the Summer Sun Celebration, **Twilight** learns that she needs friends to defeat **Nightmare Moon** and save Equestria. With her friends help, they each discover their Elements of Harmony and become the '**Mane Six**'.

Fun Fact!

Twilight and her best friends write all their adventures in the Friendship Journal.

4

With Equestria saved, **Twilight** gets to know her new friends and learns that although they are all different, they are united by their passion for friendship. Together they explore Ponyville and help everypony they meet on their adventures. **Twilight** shares all of her friendship lessons with **Princess Celestia** back in Canterlot.

Magical Moments from Season One

1

After being picked on for not having their cutie marks yet, **Apple Bloom, Scootaloo** and **Sweetie Belle** form the 'Cutie Mark Crusaders'.

2

When a lightning bolt strikes down a tree in Ponyville, **Applejack** and **Rarity** work together to save a Ponyville home from being flattened. Great teamwork ponies!

Rainbow Dash performs her second Sonic Rainboom when saving **Rarity** at the Best Young Flyer Competition in Cloudsdale. Go Rainbow Dash!

3

4

Applejack and **Rainbow Dash** learn to not let competitions come between their friendship when Twilight beats them in the 'Running of the Leaves' race.

Season Two

1

Discord, the Spirit of Disharmony, escapes from his stone imprisonment and the **Mane Six** set out to Canterlot to defeat him. When they arrive, they realise their **Elements of Harmony** are missing and **Discord** tricks them into going into the palace maze to find them.

2

In the maze, **Discord** separates the friends and convinces them to be the polar opposites of their usual selves. The friends are divided, but **Twilight** won't give up and leads the friends to Ponyville to find their Elements.

3

In Ponyville, **Twilight** realises that the power of their friendship is what will defeat **Discord**, not just their Elements. She unites her friends once more and they recapture Discord, turning him back into stone.

Did you know?

Queen Chrysalis almost married Twilight's brother, **Shining Armor!**

4

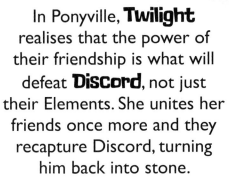

However, it isn't long until another villain tries to take over Equestria, **Queen Chrysalis.** As queen of the Changelings, she disguises herself as **Princess Cadance** and almost succeeds in taking everyponies' magic. Luckily, the **Mane Six** are there to save the day.

Magical Moments from Season Two

1

Twilight Sparkle gains a new sister-in-law when **Shining Armor** marries her childhood foalsitter, **Cadance.**

Mr and Mrs **Cake** have twins – **Pound Cake,** a Pegasus, and **Pumpkin Cake,** a Unicorn. Cute!

2

Pinkie Pie reunites long lost lovebirds, **Cranky Doodle Donkey** and **Matilda**.

3

4

Rainbow Dash discovers the exciting stories of **Daring Do** and falls in love with reading.

Season Three

1

The Crystal Empire reappears after disappearing long ago and the Mane Six are sent to help **Princess Cadance** and **Shining Armor** protect it from the evil **King Sombra.** When they arrive, they find **Cadance** is using all her magic to keep **Sombra** out and she can't hold him off for much longer.

Fun Fact!

When King Sombra tries to enter the Crystal Empire, Cadance's magic breaks his horn.

2

The friends organise a Crystal Fair to help raise the spirits of the Crystal Ponies and to keep **Sombra** out. But they soon realise that **Sombra** will be able to get into the empire as long as the Crystal Heart, which holds the empire's magic, is missing.

3

Twilight and **Spike** set off to find the heart but when Twilight is caught in **Sombra's** trap, it is up to Spike and **Cadance** to restore the heart to its home. The Crystal Ponies fill the heart with their love, recreating the protective spell on the empire and obliterating **King Sombra.**

Did you know?

The **Mane Six** help **Discord** to become good again and free him from his stone prison.

4

With the Crystal Empire safe, **Twilight** faces her toughest mission yet – to figure out an unfinished spell by **Star Swirl the Bearded.** When **Twilight** passes the test, she is given her wings and becomes an Alicorn, meaning she will be crowned a Princess!

Magical Moments from Season Three

1

Pinkie Pie finds a Mirror Pool and accidently clones herself hundreds of times!

2

Rainbow Dash is accepted into the Wonderbolt Academy. Go, Rainbow!

22

3

The ponies mistake a tourist for **Ms Harshwhinny**, who has come to inspect the Crystal Empire as a venue for the next Equestria Games – whoops!

4

Twilight accidently switches the cutie marks of her friends, resulting in confusion and accidents.

Season Four

1

Twilight's friends are helping her to adjust to her new wings and Princess duties as she prepares for the Summer Sun Celebration. But something strange is happening in Equestria, black vines are covering the land and wreaking havoc on Equestria.

Fun Fact!

When **Twilight** drinks **Zecora's** potion she sees the moment **Celestia** had to banish her sister, then called **Nightmare Moon**.

2

Twilight enlists **Discord** to help her solve the mystery, and after drinking one of **Zecora's** potions, she has a vision of the Tree of Harmony and realises it needs help. The ponies place their Elements back in the Tree of Harmony and it sprouts a flower containing a locked chest with six keyholes.

Did you know?

Twilight's castle is called the Castle of Friendship.

3

With the black vines defeated, **Discord** admits to having sown the seeds that grew the vines when he was a villain. He didn't tell **Twilight** so that she had a chance to learn how to be a leader by herself. **Twilight** forgives him and the Summer Sun Celebration commences.

4

But harmony is not restored in Ponyville for long as **Lord Tirek** arrives to take everyponies magic. Helped by **Discord**, he stops the Tree of Harmony's magic, but when the **Mane Six** solve the chests' riddle, order is restored and **Twilight** recieves her very own Castle!

Magical Moments from Season Four

1

Spike becomes a hero in the Crystal Empire after he is asked to light the torch at the opening ceremony of the Equestria Games.

Spike also accidently sends himself and the **Mane Six** into the world of his comic book, 'Power Ponies'. As side-kick, **Hum Drum**, he helps the ponies defeat supervillain, **Mane-iac**.

2

3

The keys needed to open the Chest of Harmony are objects the **Mane Six** were given after they demonstrated their Element of Harmony trait.

4

Pinkie introduces her sister, **Maud**, to the group. **Maud** has a pet rock named **Boulder**.

Season Five

1

Did you know?

Starlight Glimmer's cutie mark is a purple and white star with two glimmering streams.

In her new castle, **Princess Twilight** and her friends discover a map that alerts them to friendship problems across Equestria. They follow the map to a town where everypony has the same cutie mark — an equal sign. The town is led by **Starlight Glimmer,** who explains all ponies are equal in their town.

2

Suspecting that not everypony feels the same, the **Mane Six** investigate and find a vault where the cutie marks are kept. In the vault, the friends are lured into a trap and **Starlight Glimmer** takes their cutie marks!

3

Fluttershy discovers that Starlight hasn't given up her cutie mark, but has covered it with makeup. She exposes Starlight by splashing water on her and Starlight escapes. But the townsponies take their cutie marks back and the Mane Six have their individuality again.

Fun Fact!

The Cutie Mark Crusaders finally get their cutie marks!

4

Princess Twilight faces Starlight Glimmer again when she comes back to take revenge. With the help of Spike, Twilight reforms Starlight and takes her on as her own student to learn the Magic of Friendship.

Magical Moments from Season Five

1

Discord does not approve of **Fluttershy's** new friend, **Tree Hugger**, but he eventually learns that jealousy will not bring friends closer.

2

Pinkie Pie struggles to keep the biggest secret ever! **Princess Cadance** and **Prince Shining Armor** are going to have a baby!

3

Twilight reconciles with an old friend from Canterlot, **Moon Dancer**.

4

Countess Coloratura visits Sweet Apple Acres and reconnects with old friend, **Applejack**. But 'Rara' seems quite different to how she remembers her.

Season Six

1

Twilight Sparkle and her friends are invited to the Crystal Empire to attend the Crystalling of **Princess Cadance** and **Shining Armor's** foal. Twilight brings **Starlight Glimmer,** so that she can reconnect with her old friend **Sunburst** as part of her friendship lessons.

Fun Fact!

Starlight Glimmer becomes friends with **Trixie Lulamoon.**

2

Starlight is reluctant to meet **Sunburst**, not wanting to reveal her villainous past. Meanwhile, **Twilight** is shocked to discover her new niece is a powerful Alicorn. So powerful that her cries shatter the Crystal Heart.

3

The ponies desperately search for a spell to fix the heart, but in the end, it is fixed by **Sunburst** and **Starlight** when they finally tell each other about their past mistakes. With the Crystal Heart repaired, the new foal is named **Flurry Heart.**

4

Starlight Glimmer faces more challenges when the Changelings take over Equestria. Brave **Thorax** helps her stand up to **Queen Chrysalis** and together they convince the other Changelings that sharing love is better than taking it.

Did you know?

When brave **Thorax** gives his love freely, a huge burst of energy changes him into his new form. When the other Changelings do the same, they change too!

Magical Moments from Season Six

1

Gabby becomes an honorary member of the **Cutie Mark Crusaders.**

2

Princess Luna can enter otherponies' dreams to help with nightmares or to send a warning. She warns **Starlight Glimmer** when **Queen Chrysalis** attacks Ponyville.

34

3

Ember becomes Dragon Lord of Dragon Lands after her and **Spike** claim the sceptre in the Gauntlet of Fire.

4

Old friends **Starlight** and **Sunburst** are reunited and realise how much they missed each other.

Season Seven

1

Starlight Glimmer, Trixie, **Thorax** and **Discord** are awarded medals of honour for defeating **Queen Chrysalis**. **Twilight** realises that this means that she has taught **Starlight** all there is to know about friendship and announces her graduation. **Starlight**, now following her own path, chooses to stay in Ponyville to help her friends.

Fun Fact!

Starlight Glimmer discovers how **Star Swirl** trapped the **Pony of Shadows** by deciphering his bad horn writing.

2

Sunburst is settling into Crystal Empire when he discovers a secret diary belonging to **Star Swirl**, one of the **Pillars of Equestria**. Along with **Starlight Glimmer** and the **Mane Six**, Sunburst discovers that the Pillars are still alive and stuck in limbo with the **Pony of Shadows**.

3

Twilight convinces the ponies that it's time to free them from limbo. Using the **Pillar's** artefacts and magic she manages to release the six Pillars but accidentally frees the **Pony of Shadows** too.

Did you know?

Twilight publishes the Friendship Journal so that all creatures can become better friends.

4

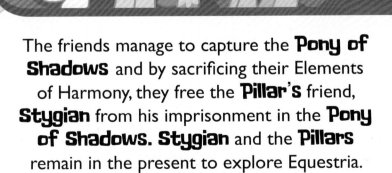

The friends manage to capture the **Pony of Shadows** and by sacrificing their Elements of Harmony, they free the **Pillar's** friend, **Stygian** from his imprisonment in the **Pony of Shadows**. **Stygian** and the **Pillars** remain in the present to explore Equestria.

Magical Moments from Season Seven

1

When **Princess Celestia** and **Princess Luna** argue about whose royal duties are more difficult, **Starlight Glimmer** swaps their cutie marks, so that they appreciate each other's roles.

2

Maud Pie earns her 'rocktorate' in Rock Science.

3

Applejack, Rarity and Rainbow Dash share stories of their favourite heroes, Rockhoof, Mistmane and Flash Magnus, with the Cutie Mark Crusaders.

4

Prince Rutherford makes Pinkie Pie an honorary Yak after she helps them dig their village out of the snow.

MY LITTLE PONY: THE MOVIE

1

Twilight Sparkle is preparing for the first ever Friendship Festival when an army invades Canterlot. The army is led by a broken-horned Unicorn called **Tempest Shadow,** who uses magical orbs to turn **Celestia, Luna** and **Cadance** to stone. **Tempest Shadow** is working for the **Storm King** who wants to steal the princesses magic.

Fun Fact!

Tempest's broken horn may weaken her magic, but she can create amazing fireworks with it!

2

Just before she is turned to stone, **Princess Celestia** tells **Twilight** to get help from "queen of the hippo". Twilight and her friends escape the invasion and travel to the desert city of Klugetown looking for this mysterious "hippo".

3

In Klugetown they meet feline con artist, **Capper** and discover that 'hippos' are Hippogriffs who live in Mount Aris. The ponies manage to board a delivery airship to take them to Mount Aris, but when **Rainbow Dash** performs a Sonic Rainboom for the ship's crew, **Tempest** spots them and chases after them, destroying their ship.

Did you know?

Capper may be a con artist, but he used to be an aristocrat and is a good friend to the ponies.

4

The ponies escape and make it to Mount Aris, but find it deserted. While exploring the ruins of the kingdom, they become trapped in an underwater cavern and are saved by a Seapony, **Princess Skystar**. **Skystar** leads them to her underwater home, Seaquestria.

5

Skystar explains that she used to be a Hippogriff, but when the **Storm King** invaded their lands, her mother, **Queen Novo,** used a magic pearl to transform all the Hippogriff's into Seaponies. Realising it could help save Equestria, **Twilight** attempts to steal the pearl, but is caught and the friends are banished to the surface.

Did you know?

After the **Storm King's** defeat, **Queen Novo** splits the pearl into hundreds of pieces, so that her people can travel between Mount Aris and Seaquestria.

6

Upset with **Twilight** for her dishonesty, her friends leave her, and **Twilight** is kidnapped by **Tempest Shadow** and brought to the **Storm King** to have her magic taken. On route, Twilight befriends **Tempest Shadow,** learning that she was outcast from her friends after her horn was broken as a filly. The **Storm King** had promised to fix it for her.

7

Meanwhile, **Spike** notices **Twilight** has been captured, and **Capper, Princess Skystar** and the rest of the **Mane Six**, all head to Canterlot to save her. To stop them from getting to her, **Storm King** conjures a tornado, trapping **Tempest**. Twilight saves her and in return **Tempest** saves **Twilight** from being petrified when **Storm King** throws an orb at her.

Fun Fact!

The biggest popstar in Equestria, **Songbird Serenade**, performs at the Friendship Festival.

8

The **Storm King's** body is petrified because of **Tempest's** sacrifice and he falls and shatters. The ponies use the **Storm King's** magic to revive **Tempest** and return the Princesses' magic to them. The Friendship Festival is celebrated with the new friends the **Mane Six** have made on their adventure.

Season Eight

1

Twilight has decided to open a School of Friendship and everycreature from all over Equestria is welcome. The new students initially enjoy school, but soon grow bored of the lessons that are being taught as requirements of the Equestria Education Association (EEA) and the six of them decide to skip class.

When **Chancellor Neighsay**, head of the EEA, pays a visit to the school, he witnesses the six creatures' chaotic return to school. After seeing non-ponies are enrolled at the scholl, he closes the school down. Convinced by **Starlight Glimmer** not to give up, **Twilight** attempts to open the school again, but finds the pupils have run away from home and are being attacked by a group of Pukwudgies.

2

3

After **Twilight** and her friends rescue the students, they reopen the school. The EEA is unhappy, but she tells them that as Princess of Friendship it is important that the school exists and she writes her own rules on how it should be run.

Did you know?

The School of Friendship is the first school to educate lots of different creatures from all over Equestria.

4

The School of Friendship is a success and the new students' friendships prove useful when **Cozy Glow,** the evil but adorable student, plans to take over as Empress of Friendship. The new friends defeat **Cozy Glow**, saving the school.

Magical Moments from Season Eight

1

When **Spike** starts moulting, he's worried he is sick. But eventually, his itchy scales recover and he finally gets his dragon wings!

2

Princess Celestia is good at almost everything, but she is terrible at acting!

3

Terramar finds it hard to decide whether to live with his Hippogriff dad in Mount Aris or his Seapony mum in Seaquestria. But the Cutie Mark Crusaders show him that it's okay to share his time with both.

4

Pinkie Pie is introduced to Maud's boyfriend, Mudbriar.

MY LITTLE PONY: Best Gift Ever

1

The ponies are preparing for Hearth's Warming Eve, but **Twilight** is worried about how much she has to get done. **Applejack** suggests they hold a 'Hearths Warming Helper' so that each of them only has to find a gift for one friend.

Fun Fact!

Princess Cadance, Shining Armor and Princess Flurry Heart spend the holiday with **Twilight.**

2

Twilight decides to make **Pinkie Pie** a legendary magic pudding. The pudding is dangerous if not prepared correctly and boils over when **Flurry Heart,** who is visiting with her parents for the holiday, adds extra ingredients.

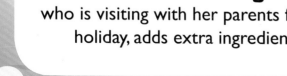

3

Pinkie Pie travels to the Artic North where her good friend, **Prince Rutherford** told her she could find the best gift. In the north, she meets a trio of magical reindeer, the 'Gift Givers of the Grove' who give her the perfect present.

Did you know?

The Gift Givers of the Grove are called **Aurora, Bori** and **Alice.**

4

Rarity orders a special hat for **Applejack,** but it is mistakenly delivered to Sweet Acorn Orchard. When she arrives to collect it, the farmers think that the gift was for their son **Pistachio**, a budding fashion designer. Rarity insists that he keep it.

5

Spike swaps his name with **Fluttershy** so that he can get **Rarity** a gift. He tries to make her a gift himself to impress her, but falls asleep after several failed attempts.

Fun Fact!

When **Pistachio** meets **Rarity** he is over the moon! She's his style icon.

6

Fluttershy, now buying a gift for **Rainbow Dash,** goes with **Applejack** to Rainbow Falls. At the market she is tricked by a disguised **Flim** and **Flam** into buying a badly made doll. Applejack helps her expose the crooks, but they have lost their gift money.

?

Discord is helping Rainbow Dash to get Fluttershy a cute creature called a Winterchilla. Rainbow Dash catches one without realising that it turns into a monstrous Winterzilla after dark!

Did you know?

Spike sings a song on his homemade guitar as his gift to Rarity.

8

When the friends exchange gifts, everything goes wrong! The pudding overflows and the Winterzilla scares them. Luckily, Pinkie Pie's perfect gift is the pudding's missing ingredients and Fluttershy calms the Winterzilla. The friends realise that the greatest gift they can give is their friendship.

Season Nine

1

Princesses **Celestia** and **Luna** summon the **Mane Six** to Equestria to ask that they take over the throne when they retire. **Twilight** is not sure about taking their place, but before she can, danger threatens Equestria. **Grogar**, a fearsome legend, has summoned a group of villians to conquer Equestria!

Did you know?

Grogar's uses his magical orb to help him cast spells and keep tabs on the **Mane Six.**

2

First, **King Sombra** attacks, destroying the Tree of Harmony and the Elements it holds. With the tree destroyed, the Everfree Forest grows out of hand and overruns Ponyville. **Princesses Celestia** and **Luna** team up with **Star Swirl** to maintain the forest whilst the **Mane Six** confront **King Sombra** in Canterlot.

3

With **Discord's** help the ponies battle **King Sombra,** but when **Discord** is badly hurt, they fear the evil king will win. Realising that they don't need their Elements to defeat **King Sombra,** the six friends harness the Magic of Friendship to take **Sombra** down, once and for all.

Fun Fact!

Lord Tirek, Queen Chrysalis and Cozy Glow actually become good friends when they team up to defeat Twilight Sparkle.

4

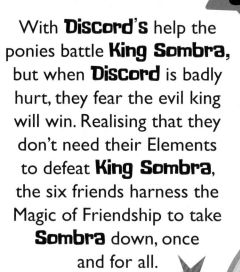

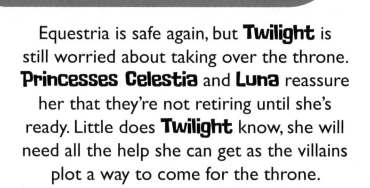

Equestria is safe again, but **Twilight** is still worried about taking over the throne. **Princesses Celestia** and **Luna** reassure her that they're not retiring until she's ready. Little does **Twilight** know, she will need all the help she can get as the villains plot a way to come for the throne.

Magical Moments from Season Nine

1

The Young Six try to repair the Tree of Harmony, but when they can't, they build a magical treehouse instead.

Scootaloo faces a big decision when her parents announce they want to move to Shirelanka.

2

3

Fluttershy and **Angel Bunny** swap bodies after drinking one of **Zecora's** potions!

4

Sugar Belle and **Big Mac** propose to each other at the same time! They both say Eeeyup!

MY LITTLE PONY:
Rainbow Roadtrip

1

The **Mane Six** go on a road trip to Hope Hollow where **Rainbow Dash** is the guest of honour at the Rainbow Festival. But when they arrive, they notice that the town isn't as colourful as they expected, and every pony is grey!

Fun Fact!

Petunia Petals is the town's librarian, Hotel Receptionist and tour guide. Is there anything she doesn't do?

2

Confused as to why there is no colour in the town, the ponies' new friend, **Petunia Petals** tells them to meet with the mayor to find out what happened. **Mayor Sunny Skies** reluctantly admits that there is no Rainbow Festival and he lied to get them to come to town.

3

Mayor Sunny explains that back when his **Grandpa Skies** was mayor, Hope Hollow was full of colour, but over time the ponies became less interested in one another. Mayor Sunny tried to bring the ponies together with a Rainbow Generator, but instead of producing a rainbow it sucked up all the town's colour instead.

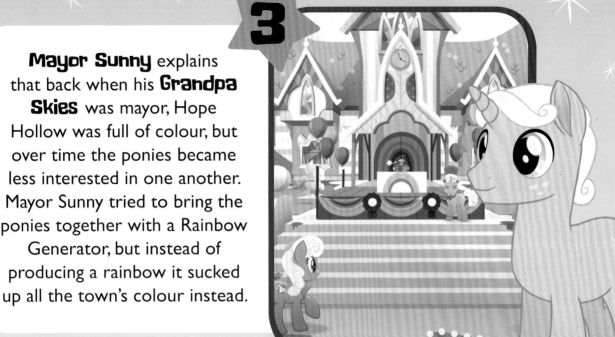

Did you know?

Hope Hollow used to have a Rainbow Festival every year, with a big rainbow which filled the sky!

4

Twilight and her friends decide to stay in Hope Hollow and help **Mayor Sunny** put on the Rainbow Festival. **Applejack** helps handi-pony **Torque Wrench** fix the Rainbow Generator, **Pinkie Pie** and **Fluttershy** head to the bakery to get the food for the celebration, **Rarity** gets the town spruced up, and **Twilight** and **Applejack** work on reversing the spell that took the town's colour away.

5

Twilight tries lots of different spells to get the generator to work, but she still can't get the colour to come back. Whilst she's working, **Rainbow Dash** meets siblings **Barley** and **Pickle**, a flying duo who are her biggest fans. **Dash** agrees to teach them her tricks so that they can put on an air show at the festival.

Fun Fact!

Barley and **Pickle** spend more time arguing than flying, until they meet **Rainbow Dash**.

6

Across the town, the other ponies are making friends. **Rarity** helps a budding fashion designer create a new collection, **Pinkie** and **Fluttershy** reunite **Mr and Mrs Hoofington** with their neighbour **Moody Root**, and **Applejack** even convinces grumpy **Torque Wrench** to be her friend.

7

The ponies don't notice, but as they make friends in Hope Hollow, bits of colour come back to the town. Everypony comes to the festival and **Applejack** points out that the colour's coming back.

Did you know?

Mayor Sunny Skies proposes to **Petunia Petals.** She says YES!

8

Mayor Sunny Skies opens the festival with the newly fixed Rainbow Generator. With the townspeople back together, the generator has enough power to produce a huge rainbow over the town. Hope Hollow is once again full of colour and friendship.

Meet the Mane Characters

Rainbow Dash

Applejack

Twilight Sparkle

Twilight Sparkle

Species: Alicorn

Element of Harmony: Magic

Job: Headmare at the School of Friendship, Princess of Friendship

Lives in: Castle of Friendship, Ponyville

Hobbies: Reading, learning, mentoring her students

Dislikes: Surprises, forces that threaten Equestria

Family: Princess Flurry Heart (Niece), Twilight Velvet (Mother), Night Light (Father), Shining Armor (Brother)

Friends: The Mane Six, Starlight Glimmer, Spike

Cutie Mark:

True Friend!
Obsessed with planning and organising, **Twilight** can sometimes get frazzled. It's a good thing **Spike** is there to help her.

Fun Fact!
Twilight got her cutie mark after she hatched **Spike** from an egg.

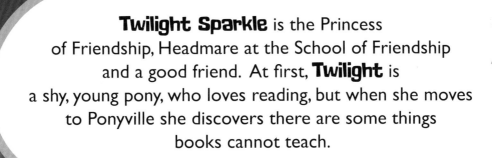

Twilight Sparkle is the Princess of Friendship, Headmare at the School of Friendship and a good friend. At first, **Twilight** is a shy, young pony, who loves reading, but when she moves to Ponyville she discovers there are some things books cannot teach.

Twilight's first home in Ponyville is the Golden Oak Library.

Twilight travels around Equestria in her purple hot air balloon.

Spike is **Twilight's** assistant and best friend. She also has a pet owl, **Owlowicious**, to keep her company when studying at night.

Twilight Sparkle's Other Forms

Breezy Twilight

Twilight transforms herself into a Breezy to help guide the Breezies back on their flight path.

Seapony Twilight

Queen Novo transforms Twilight and her friends when they visit Seaquestria.

Star Swirl Twilight

She dresses up in costume as her hero, the legendary Star Swirl the Bearded for Nightmare Night.

We know that **Twilight** gets her wings in Season Three and becomes an Alicorn, but she goes through many more transformations and disguises. Here are some of her favourites.

Camo Twilight
Twilight tries to blend in whilst watching the dragon migration.

Which of Twilight's costumes is your favourite?

Clown Twilight
She runs away from a crowd of ponies by disguising herself as a clown.

Superhero Twilight
She transforms into a superhero when she's sucked into Spike's comic book, 'Power Ponies' and defeats Mane-iac.

From the beginning ...

Twilight Sparkle

Follow Twilight Sparkle from Season One to Season Nine of *MY LITTLE PONY: Friendship is Magic*.

1 **Twilight** begins her friendship lessons in Ponyville and learns that any problem can be solved with some help from her friends.

2 Now she understands the value of friendship, **Twilight** settles in Ponyville. She is the first to spot something is wrong when **Chrysalis** tries to impersonate **Cadance**.

3 **Twilight** solves **Star Swirl's** unfinished spell and gets her wings, making her an Alicorn and a Princess.

4 **Twilight** is worried that **Rainbow Dash** is unprepared for her exam to join the **Wonderbolts**, so she persuades the town to help **Dash** study.

5

When her friends have a fun weekend with **Discord**, **Twilight** admits that she is jealous they had fun without her. Her friends show her that they are still as much her friend as **Discord's**.

6

With a reformed **Starlight** as her student, **Twilight** continues to spread the values of friendship.

7

Twilight realises that **Starlight** has excelled at her friendship lessons and no longer needs her guidance. She turns to **Celestia** for advice and realises the hardest lesson is letting **Starlight** go.

8

Twilight opens the School of Friendship and welcomes everycreature from all over Equestria to learn the magic of friendship.

9

Princess Celestia and **Princess Luna** are retiring and it's up to **Twilight** to reign over Equestria. She's scared she won't be ready, but her friends show her that she has learnt far more than she realises.

Castle of Friendship

Did you know? →

The roots of the Golden Oak Library hang as a chandelier in the throne room.

Fun Fact!

The castle is made of crystal and looks just like a treehouse.

After a fire destroyed the Golden Oak Library, **Twilight's** new home emerges on the outskirts of Ponyville at the end of Season Four. From Season Six, **Starlight Glimmer** moves in and joins **Twilight** and **Spike.**

The Cutie Map, a 3D interactive map of Equestria, sits inside the throne room.

Pinkie Pie

Species: Earth Pony

Element of Harmony: Laughter

Job: Teacher at the School of Friendship, baker at Sugarcube Corner Bakery

Lives in: Above Sugarcube Corner Bakery in Ponyville

Hobbies: Party planning, baking and telling jokes

Dislikes: Keeping secrets

Family: Maud Pie (Sister), Marble Pie (Sister), Limestone Pie (Sister), Cloudy Quartz (Mother), Igneous Rock Pie (Father)

Friends: The Mane Six, Gummy, Prince Rutherford

Cutie Mark:

Her full name is **Pinkamena Diane Pie.**

Pinkie Pie is the most energetic and fun pony EVER! She loves nothing more than baking cakes and throwing parties for her many friends. Though she may seem goofy, **Pinkie Pie** has a big heart and cares about everycreature she meets.

True Friend!

Although she's very different from the rest of the Pie family, **Pinkie** always makes time for them and they love her for who she is.

Fun Fact!

Pinkie Pie grew up on Rock Farm!

Pinkie Pie's Other Forms

Performing Pinkie

Pinkie loves to perform and put on shows for her friends, making everypony laugh.

Seapony Pinkie

To visit her friends in Seaquestria, Pinkie transforms into a Seapony.

Which of Pinkie's disguises is the best?

Detective Pinkie

Solving mysteries with her friends.

Pinkie Pie loves to dress up for parties. She also has some interesting and unusual disguises. Here are some of her favourites.

Cheerleader Pinkie

Dressed from head to hoof in ribbons and pompoms, Pinkie Pie is everypony's biggest fan.

Chicken Pinkie

Pinkie has a unique Nightmare Night costume, ready for trick-or-treating.

Zom-bee Pinkie

When Rainbow Dash plays a prank on her friends, Pinkie Pie pretends to turn into a Rainbow zom-bee to get her back.

From the beginning ...

Pinkie Pie

Follow Pinkie Pie from Season One to Season Nine of *MY LITTLE PONY: Friendship is Magic.*

1 Pinkie Pie welcomed Twilight to Ponyville with a huge surprise party, and though Twilight was overwhelmed at first, Pinkie's positivity won her round.

2 Pinkie is put in charge of getting the Cake's dessert to a competition in Canterlot, but before she gets there, part of the dessert is eaten!

3 Pinkie Pie is torn between spending time with all her friends and learns the hard way that there can be too many Pinkies!

4 When another party-planner, Cheese Sandwich, arrives in Ponyville, Pinkie Pie is disappointed. Eventually she learns that she can work with Cheese Sandwich to throw Rainbow Dash the best party ever!

5 Pinkie helps the Griffons to be nicer to one another and makes peace between the Ponies and the Yaks. She also finds it almost impossible to keep Princess Cadance and Prince Shining Armor's big news a secret!

6 Pinkie and her friends are sick of Rainbow Dash's tricks, so they pretend her latest joke has gone wrong and made them all into Rainbow Zom-bees.

7 Pinkie convinces her sister Maud to move to Ponyville. Now they can hang out all the time!

8 Pinkie takes up the yovidaphone, a popular instrument in Yakyakistan, but her playing isn't very good.

9 Pinkie Pie discovers that her life's purpose is to make everypony laugh after she helps Cheese Sandwich regain his smile.

Sugarcube Corner

Fun Fact!

Pinkie Pie works in the bakery, making pies, sweets and cupcakes for everypony.

The bakery looks as though it's been made out of sweets and gingerbread.

Mr and Mrs Cake run Sugarcube Corner, Ponyville's super sweet bakery.

Inside is the perfect space for throwing parties, dancing and firing a confetti canon!

Did you know?

Pinkie Pie lives above the bakery with her pet alligator, **Gummy.**

Rainbow Dash

Species: Pegasus Pony

Element of Harmony: Loyalty

Job: Teacher at the School of Friendship, member of the Wonderbolts

Lives in: Cloudomonium, over Ponyville

Hobbies: Flying and racing

Dislikes: Being beaten

Family: Windy Whistles (Mother), Bow Hothoof (Father)

Friends: The Mane Six, Tank, Gilda the Griffon

Cutie Mark:

Although **Tank** isn't the speediest of pets, he once saved **Rainbow Dash** from a rockslide, so she values his loyalty.

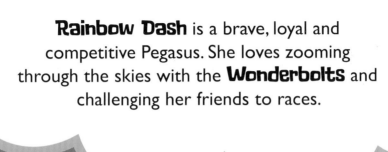

Rainbow Dash is a brave, loyal and competitive Pegasus. She loves zooming through the skies with the **Wonderbolts** and challenging her friends to races.

True Friend!

Rainbow reads lots of Daring Do's adventure novels and has helped the real **Daring Do, A.K.Yearling**, defeat the villains that inspire the stories.

Fun Fact!

Her custom move is the sonic rainboom.

Her parents are her biggest fans! Sometimes they can be a little too enthusiastic.

Rainbow Dash's Other Forms

Wonderbolt
Rainbow Dash has always dreamt of joining the **Wonderbolts**. And doesn't she look great in her uniform?

Seapony
Now Dash can see just how fast she can swim!

Zapp
Dash dresses up as Zapp to help defeat Mane-iac in 'Power Ponies'.

Adventurous Rainbow Dash always wants the best disguises and costumes. Here are some of her favourites.

Which outfit does Rainbow Dash look coolest in?

Teacher Dash
Dressed for success, Rainbow Dash wants to be the best teacher there ever was.

Faded Rainbow Dash
When **Discord** hypnotises the Pegasus. Dash forgets her friends and is drained of colour.

Rainbow Dash
Dresses up as a **Shadowbolt** for Nightmare Night.

From the beginning ...

Rainbow Dash

Follow Rainbow Dash from Season One to Season Nine of *MY LITTLE PONY: Friendship is Magic.*

1 We first meet **Rainbow Dash**, the most loyal pony and the best flyer in all of Ponyville, as she soars through the clouds above the town.

2 But **Dash's** need for speed means she can be a bit too competitive. When she meets **Tank**, the loyal tortoise, she learns there are more important qualities in friendship.

3 **Dash** realises her dream of training with the **Wonderbolts**. But she also learns that loyalty and teamwork are just as important as speed and ability.

4 When **Rainbow Dash** has to choose a team to join for the Equestria Games try-outs, her loyalty is put to the ultimate test.

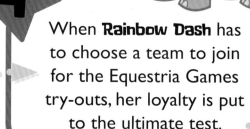

5

Dash realises it's okay to find things hard and that friends can help you when times are tough.

6

When **Dash**'s jokes nose-dive, she learns that not everypony likes her tricks. She must pay more attention to other ponies' feelings.

7

Rainbow Dash meets her hero, **Flash Magnus**, who inspired her to become totally awesome.

8

Now a teacher at the School of Friendship, **Rainbow Dash** wants her students to be the best. Still as competitive as ever, she prepares them for all sorts of challenges, which proves very useful when **Cozy Glow** turns up!

9

Now **Rainbow Dash** must use her confidence to help **Twilight** prepare to reign over Equestria. Her energy and loyalty make her the perfect pony for the job.

Cloudsdale

Only Pegasi can reach Cloudsdale. That is, unless they have an Alicorn friend, like **Twilight**, to cast a spell that helps them walk on clouds.

Fun Fact!

Pegasus Ponies look after the weather. They kick clouds to bring out the sun, hop on clouds to make it rain and mix rainbows.

Welcome to Cloudsdale, home for many Pegasus Ponies. Just north of Ponyville, the city of clouds contains a weather factory, a stadium called the Cloudaseum and the Wonderbolts academy.

How many jars are in the weather factory?

In the weather factory, Pegasus Ponies store the snowflakes and lightning bolts they have crafted.

Fluttershy

- **Species:** Pegasus Pony
- **Element of Harmony:** Kindness
- **Job:** Teacher at the School of Friendship and singer in the Pony Tones
- **Lives in:** Cottage at the edge of the Everfree Forest
- **Hobbies:** Singing and caring for animals
- **Dislikes:** Rudeness
- **Family:** Mrs Shy (Mother), Mr Shy (Father), Zephyr Breeze (Brother)
- **Friends:** The Mane Six, Angel Bunny, Discord, Tree Hugger
- **Cutie Mark:**

Did you know?

Fluttershy can talk to all animals.

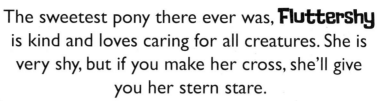

The sweetest pony there ever was, **Fluttershy** is kind and loves caring for all creatures. She is very shy, but if you make her cross, she'll give you her stern stare.

Fluttershy builds an animal sanctuary to help sick animals recover and thrive.

True Friend!

Though she is very shy, Fluttershy can show her angry side. When she does, she sticks up for her friends and has even taken on a dragon.

She is very musical and enjoys singing and conducting choirs of birds and woodland creatures.

Fluttershy's Other Forms

Flutterbat
When the ponies accidentally turn Fluttershy into a Flutterbat, they have to use **Applejack's** fruit to catch her.

Seapony Fluttershy
Fluttershy loves meeting the Seaponies in Seaquestria.

Spy Fluttershy
The perfect agent, Fluttershy shows how brave she is during her secret mission to help **Twilight**.

Though **Fluttershy** may seem quiet and shy, she is full of surprises. When she dresses up her personality can sometimes change drastically!

Pony Tones Fluttershy
Despite her shyness, Fluttershy shines as a singer with the Pony Tones.

Saddle Rager Fluttershy
Do NOT make Fluttershy angry or she'll turn into a huge muscular monster!

From the beginning ...

Fluttershy

Follow Fluttershy from Season One to Season Nine of *MY LITTLE PONY: Friendship is Magic.*

1 **Fluttershy** is introduced as a shy and kind pony who feels more comfortable talking to animals than ponies.

2 Although she gets nervous, **Fluttershy** isn't afraid to use tough love when it's needed. She faces her fears and shows how strong she can be.

3 **Fluttershy** uses kindness to solve problems. By continuing to offer friendship to **Discord**, she convinces him to use his powers for good.

4 Shy and quiet **Fluttershy** steps in for a performance with vocal quartet the Pony Tones and finds a love for performing.

5

Once the cutie map appears, **Fluttershy** is sent on a mission to the Smokey Mountains to solve a friendship problem and rescue animals' habitats.

6

We meet **Fluttershy**'s brother, **Zephyr Breeze**, for the first time and **Fluttershy** must use her tough love once more.

7

Fluttershy realises her dream of opening a wildlife haven, Sweet Feather Sanctuary.

8

Now a teacher at the School of Friendship, **Fluttershy**'s adventures include saving the Kirin village from a vow of silence, looking after Rarity's Manehatten boutique and helping to defeat sweet-but-evil **Cozy Glow**.

9

Fluttershy learns to take more time for her friends, especially **Angel Bunny**, when **Zecora** switches their bodies around!

Fluttershy's Cottage

Fun Fact!

The cottage has birdhouses and animal burrows for animals to stay.

Building the sanctuary was hard work. **Wrangler, Hard Hat** and **Dandy Grandeur** all helped.

Did you know?

Even though **Fluttershy** is a Pegasus Pony, she prefers to live on the ground, surrounded by the forest.

Fluttershy lives on the edge of the Everfree Forest with her pet bunny, **Angel** and many other animal friends. With the help of her friends and **Dr Fauna**, Fluttershy builds a sanctuary for sick or lonely animals. She calls it the Sweet Feather Sanctuary.

Sweet Feather Sanctuary has a waterfall, a treehouse and lots of grassy areas.

Rarity

Species: Unicorn

Element of Harmony: Generosity

Job: Teacher at the School of Friendship and owner of Fashion Boutiques across Equestria

Lives in: Carousel Boutique, Ponyville

Hobbies: Designing outfits for everypony, eating ice cream and performing with the Pony Tones

Dislikes: Bad manners and camping

Family: Sweetie Belle (Sister), Cookie Crumbles (Mother), Hondo Flanks (Father)

Friends: Spike, The Mane Six, Sassy Saddles, Miss Pommel

Cutie Mark:

Rarity is a fabulous Unicorn with a love of fashion. She adores creating new outfits and making everypony feel special.

Suri Polomare steals **Rarity's** design but **Rarity** still remains generous with everypony.

Rarity is a great big sister. She makes **Sweetie Belle** costumes for her plays and always has time to spend with her.

True Friend!

Rarity cuts off her own tail to help sea serpent, **Stephen Magnet,** feel better about himself.

Did you know?

Rarity has a pet Persian cat called **Opalescence.** Although sometimes grumpy, Opal is a great comfort to Rarity when she is designing clothes.

Rarity's Other Forms

Seapony Rarity

Rarity loves the elegance of having a tail, when she's a Seapony.

Teacher Rarity

Ready to teach everycreature the secret to fashion!

96

Rarity loves to style herself and her friends in the finest couture, but she'll also dress up in silly outfits with her pony pals. Here are some of her best looks.

Ball Rarity
Nothing makes her happier than finding the perfect outfit for the Grand Galloping Gala.

Which is Rarity's most elegant outfit?

Comic book Rarity
Defeating evil genius, Mane-iac!

Secret Mission Rarity
Rarity goes undercover to find out what Flim and Flam are up to.

From the beginning ...

Rarity

Follow Rarity from Season One to Season Nine of *MY LITTLE PONY: Friendship is Magic.*

1 Fashionista **Rarity** welcomes **Twilight** to Ponyville and makes her new friend feel at home.

2 **Rarity** travels to Manehattan, dreaming of becoming Equestria's number one clothes designer.

3 **Twilight** accidently casts a spell giving **Rarity Rainbow Dash's** cutie mark and putting her in charge of weather control!

4 **Rarity** takes part in her first fashion competition and makes friends with fellow fashion designer, **Miss Pommel.**

5

Rarity successfully opens her very own fashion boutique in Canterlot and helps **Miss Pommel** to rescue Manehattan's community theatre.

6

The Manehattan branch of **Rarity**'s boutique opens and Rarity help **Sweetie Belle** to make the ultimate go cart.

7

Rarity accidentally takes a 'remover' potion from **Zecora** and loses all her mane. But with the help of her friends, she learns to rock her new look in time for a photoshoot.

8

Now a teacher at the School of Friendship, **Rarity** is passing on the secret of generosity to everycreature.

9

When **Spike** spends more time with his new friend than with her, **Rarity** learns that sometimes friendships change but they're never gone.

Manehattan

Manehattan ponies are not the most friendly of ponies, but **Rarity** wins most of them round.

Fun Fact!

Lots of musical ponies live in Manehattan, including **Songbird Serenade**, **DJ Pon-3** and **Coloratura**.

The fashion centre of Equestria, Manehattan is a busy and lively city. It's home to many fashion boutiques, restaurants and tourist attractions.

Rarity's boutique, Rarity for You, is full of stylish designs to make everypony feel special.

How many ponies can you see in Manehatten?

Did you know?

Manehattan is actually an island and you can reach it by catching the Railroad Express train over the bridge from the mainland.

Applejack

Species: Earth Pony

Element of Harmony: Honesty

Job: Apple farmer at Sweet Apple Acres, teacher at the School of Friendship

Lives in: Ponyville on Sweet Apple Acres farm

Hobbies: Tending to crops, making apple cider, planning Apple family reunions

Dislikes: Giving up

Family: Apple Bloom (sister), Big McIntosh (brother), Granny Smith (grandma)

Friends: Mane Six, Gilda, Coloratura, Winona

Cutie Mark: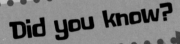

Did you know? ➤

Applejack loves music and plays the fiddle, the banjo and the flute!

Applejack is the hardest working pony in Equestria. She is very close to her family and is always helping on the farm. Her competitiveness can get the best of her, but she has the biggest heart and values honesty in everypony.

The **Apple family** is the biggest family in Equestria and the original founders of Ponyville.

Winona is **Applejack's** pet dog.

True Friend!

Applejack is a protective older sister, and this sometimes annoys **Apple Bloom**, but it's only because she wants the best for her.

103

Applejack's Other Forms

Breezie Applejack
Guiding the Breezies home.

Seapony Applejack
Applejack loves having a tail so that she can race Rainbow Dash around Seaquestria.

Scarecrow Applejack
Her favourite Nightmare Night costume.

Hardworking **Applejack** prefers a costume that she can get mucky in but she doesn't mind trying out some silly ones too. Here's her latest looks.

Mistress Mare-velous
Applejack's comic book alter-ego.

Mechanic Applejack
She's always happy to roll up her sleeves and get down to work.

Which of Applejack's costumes is your favourite?

From the beginning ...

Applejack

Follow Applejack from Season One to Season Nine of *MY LITTLE PONY: Friendship is Magic.*

1 **Applejack** introduces **Twilight** to the Apple farm and her family.

2 Struggling with the busy Applebuck season, **Applejack** learns that it's okay to ask for help.

3 **Applejack** plans a big Apple family reunion, saves **Spike** from a Timberwolf and help young filly, **Babs**, combat bullies.

4 Playing detective, **Applejack** discovers **Flim & Flam's** money-making schemes and encourages them to be honest.

5 **Applejack** helps **Miss Pommel** to revive her local community theatre by building a stage outside the park showcasing the theatre's talents.

6 **Applejack** is still very busy but does find time for **Buckball** and a trip to the spa with **Rarity.**

7 **Rarity** asks **Applejack** to judge a fashion competition, but **Applejack's** honesty upsets some of the contestants.

8 Teaching at the School of Friendship suits **Applejack** and she wants to be the best teacher she possibly can.

9 **Applejack** teaches **Apple Bloom** that nopony should grow out of having fun when **Apple Bloom** takes her place in the Harvest of a Hundred Moons.

Sweet Apple Acres

The big barn is perfect for family parties.

All kinds of exciting events happen on the farm, including Helping Hooves music festival.

Applejack lives and works on Sweet Apple Acres with her family. She lets little sister **Apple Bloom** use her old tree house as the **Cutie Mark Crusaders'** clubhouse.

Did you know?

It's not just apples the family grow. They also have carrots, corn and grapes.

Fun Fact!

The **CMC's** hang out at the clubhouse and help other ponies to discover their cutie marks.

Princess Celestia

Species: Alicorn

Job: Co-ruler of Equestria, with sister Luna and mentor to Twilight

Lives in: Canterlot

Hobbies: Performing in plays and eating cupcakes

Dislikes: Fighting with her sister, villains trying to take over Equestria

Family: Princess Luna (sister), Princess Cadance (adoptive niece)

Friends: Twilight (student), Philomena (pet Phoenix)

Cutie Mark:

Despite being a princess, **Celestia** loves to goof around with her friends.

True Friend!

She is very patient, but if you push her, she will use her powerful magic to defend the kingdom.

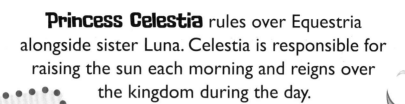

Princess Celestia rules over Equestria alongside sister Luna. Celestia is responsible for raising the sun each morning and reigns over the kingdom during the day.

Did you know?

She is a mentor to young ponies and runs the School for Gifted Unicorns, which is where she taught **Twilight**.

Discord used to rule Equestria, but nopony was happy and so **Celestia** and **Luna** defeated Discord and turned him to stone. Harmony was restored to the kingdom.

Celestia is very wise and guides **Twilight** through her adventures.

Celestia has a pet Phoenix called **Philomena**.

Both **Celestia** and **Luna** have decided it is time for them to retire from the job of ruler.

Princess Luna

Species: Alicorn

Job: Ruler of Equestria with her sister Celestia

Lives in: Canterlot

Hobbies: Helping ponies who are having nightmares and playing pranks

Dislikes: Thinking back to her days as Nightmare Moon

Family: Princess Celestia (sister)

Friends: Starlight Glimmer

Cutie Mark:

True Friend!

Luna feels guilty for her evil actions as **Nightmare Moon,** and so now works hard chasing away ponies nightmares, so that nopony feels afraid again.

Princess Luna rules over the nights in Equestria. She brings out the moon and watches over everypony, protecting the kingdom. Luna spends the night times helping ponies to have happy dreams.

Luna loves to play tricks on ponies, especially on Nightmare Night.

Luna appears in the dreams of **Sweetie Belle**, **Scootaloo** and **Apple Bloom**, helping them to face their fears.

Luna helps **Starlight Glimmer** combat her guilt for her past mistakes.

Luna once lived inside the moon, when she was banished by **Celestia**.

Canterlot

Places in Canterlot include the Library of Magic, a theatre and Cloud Stadium.

Did you know?

Canterlot is home to many rich ponies including **Fancy Pants**, **Hoity Toity** and **Photo Finish**.

Princess Celestia's magical school, the School for Gifted Unicorns is in Canterlot.

Built on the side of a mountain that overlooks Ponyville, Canterlot is the capital of Equestria. It is home to **Celestia** and **Luna** and was **Twilight's** home before she was sent to Ponyville on a friendship quest.

When **Twilight** was a student at the School for Gifted Unicorns, she lived with **Spike** in a tower in Canterlot castle.

Princess Cadance

Species: Alicorn

Job: Ruler of the Crystal Empire

Lives in: The Crystal Castle in the Crystal Empire

Hobbies: Hanging out with Twilight and going on adventures

Dislikes: Queen Chrysalis

Family: Prince Shining Armor (Husband), Flurry Heart (Daughter), Princess Celestia (adopted Aunt), Twilight Sparkle (sister-in-law)

Friends: Sunburst, Spike

Cutie Mark:

Fun Fact!

Her full name is Princess Mi Amore Cadenza.

We first meet **Princess Cadance,** at her wedding to **Shining Armor, Twilight's** brother. **Twilight** couldn't be more thrilled to have her as a sister-in-law and together they defeat the changeling, **Queen Chrysalis.** Now **Princess Cadance** is the ruler of the Crystal Empire and has a baby foal, **Princess Flurry Heart.**

Queen Chrysalis steals her identity in 'A Canterlot Wedding'.

True Friend!

Cadance used to foal-sit **Twilight** when Twilight was a filly. They have a secret hoofshake!

Cadance is kind, caring and a natural leader.

Crystal Empire

Fun Fact!

The crystal heart sits inside the Crystal Castle and its magic protects the kingdom from attacks.

Crystal ponies can only be found in the Crystal Empire. They sparkle and you can see through them. They eat crystal candy.

After disappearing for many moons, the Crystal Empire reappeared in the north of Equestria. **King Sombra** had taken over the empire and enslaved the **Crystal Ponies**. Once he was defeated, **Celestia** sent **Cadance** and **Shining Armor** to live in the Crystal Castle and look after the kingdom.

Sunburst moves to the Crystal Empire to become **Flurry Heart's** crystaller.

Did you know?

Spike helped the Crystal Ponies to defeat **King Sombra**. To thank him, the Crystal Ponies built a crystal sculpture of his heroic deed.

Spike

- **Species:** Dragon
- **Job:** Twilight Sparkle's Assistant
- **Lives in:** Castle of Friendship in Ponyville
- **Hobbies:** Eating gems, telling jokes and reading comic books
- **Dislikes:** Waking up early and feeling hungry
- **Family:** He lives with Twilight
- **Friends:** Ember the Dragon Lord, Rarity, Thorax

Fun Fact!
Spike delivers letters with his green fire breath.

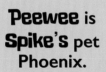

Peewee is Spike's pet Phoenix.

Spike is Twilight's best friend and loyal assistant. He loves to play pranks but also works hard to help Twilight with her friendship missions. He sometimes feels he might be missing out by living away from other dragons but Ponyville is his home and he loves hanging out with everycreature.

Spike gets his wings after going through the 'moult' in Season Eight.

Twilight hatched Spike from an egg at the School for Gifted Unicorns and they've been best friends ever since.

True Friend!

Spike gave Thorax a second chance and showed that Changelings don't have to be mean.

He has a huuuuge crush on Rarity.

Discord

Species: Draconequus

Job: Helping the Mane Six with the friendship quests (which often causes chaos)

Lives in: Chaosville

Hobbies: Attending parties, causing mischief and having tea parties with Fluttershy

Dislikes: Being left out and being bored

Friends: Fluttershy, CMCs

Discord is made up of lots of different animals. He has one antler, one horn, a bat's wing, an eagle's claw and a lizard's tail.

Fun Fact!

Discord once brought the **Smooze** as his guest to the Grand Galloping Gala.

122

Discord once ruled over Equestria, creating chaos and disharmony but **Princesses Celestia** and **Luna** defeated him and turned him to stone. The **Mane Six** worked hard to reform **Discord**, showing him that the power of friendship was more important than chaos. **Discord** became their friend and even helps out at the School of Friendship.

True Friend!

Discord acts as head of the School of Friendship when **Twilight** is called away.

Discord loves turning things upside-down, so Chaosville is his perfect home.

Top disguises:

Starlight Glimmer

Species: Unicorn

Job: Guidance Counsellor at the School of Friendship

Lives in: Ponyville, previously Our Town

Hobbies: Assisting Trixie with magic tricks and flying kites

Dislikes: She panics when she's left in charge

Family: Firelight (Father)

Friends: Trixie Lulamoon, Sunburst

Cutie Mark:

True Friend!

Sometimes, **Starlight** doubts her abilities and worries that she can't look after the school, but the friendship of the **Mane Six** always convinces her she can.

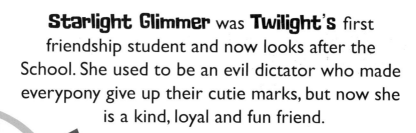

Starlight Glimmer was **Twilight's** first friendship student and now looks after the School. She used to be an evil dictator who made everypony give up their cutie marks, but now she is a kind, loyal and fun friend.

Starlight travels with 'The Great and Powerful Trixie' performing magic shows around Equestria.

Cozy Glow captures **Starlight** in a magic prison as part of her plan to take over Equestria.

Fun Fact!

Starlight's filly-friend was **Sunburst**. They grew up together in Sire's Hollow.

Starlight's dad, **Firelight**, is really supportive, and will do anything to help her.

125

School of Friendship

Cozy Glow once attended the school, pretending she just wanted to be a student, but then she tried to take over Equestria.

Fun Fact!

The **Cutie Mark Crusaders** are tutors at the school.

Chancellor Neighsay would not approve the School of Friendship because it accepts different creatures, not just ponies. So **Twilight** founded it independently.

126

Did you know? ➤

Starlight Glimmer is the school counsellor until **Twilight** asks her to take over as headmare in Season Nine.

The School of Friendship was founded by **Twilight Sparkle** to teach everycreature about the Magic of Friendship. Twilight and the **Mane Six** want to make everycreature feel welcome. They have Hippogriff, Yak, Dragon, Changeling and Griffon students as well as Ponies.

Each of the **Mane Six** teach at the school. Their classrooms represent their personalities.

Trixie Lulamoon

Species: Unicorn

Job: Travelling magician

Magic tricks: Making ponies disappear, card tricks, escaping from locked chests and creating fireworks

Hobbies: Practising magic tricks and playing pranks on everypony

Friends: Gilda, Starlight Glimmer, Thorax

Cutie Mark:

True Friend!

Trixie can still be boastful but is learning to let others share their talents, too.

Trixie Lulamoon is a Unicorn who attended **Princess Celestia's** School for Gifted Unicorns and now works as a travelling magician. She steals the Alicorn Amulet to try and prove how powerful she can be, but eventually apologises and is forgiven by **Twilight**.

Fun Fact!

The Alicorn Amulet is a legendary tool that gives the wearer strong powers, but also makes them greedy. Only the wearer can remove the amulet, so **Twilight** must convince **Trixie** to remove it herself.

Starlight Glimmer and **Trixie** were both unkind in the past, but now focus on being a friend to everypony.

Trixie travels around Equestria in a wagon. It's very cozy and contains everything she needs.

129

Gallus

Species: Griffon

Job: Student at the School of Friendship

Lives in: Griffonstone

Hobbies: Racing and flying with friends

Dislikes: Homework and being stuck in small spaces

Family: Grandpa Gruff (Grandfather)

Friends: Yona, Sandbar, Ocellus, Silverstream and Smolder

Gallus is a Griffin student at the School of Friendship. He is sarcastic and can seem a little mean, but he has a big heart and cares a lot about the **Young Six.**

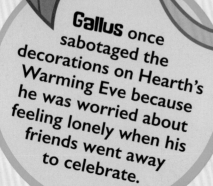

Gallus once sabotaged the decorations on Hearth's Warming Eve because he was worried about feeling lonely when his friends went away to celebrate.

Griffonstone

Griffonstone is home to **Gallus**, **Gilda** and many other Griffons. It is a town high up on a mountain and is mostly made up of shabby huts with straw roofs. Griffonstone used to be a grand city, but after the Idol of Boreas was stolen it fell into ruin.

Vacant buildings in Griffonstone include a library, the castle and a statue of King Grover in Abysmal Abyss.

Rainbow Dash and **Pinkie Pie** are sent to the town by the Cutie Map.

Silverstream

Species: Hippogriff/Seapony

Job: Student at the School of Friendship

Lives in: Seaquestria and Mount Aris

Hobbies: Learning about life and the sea

Dislikes: The Storm King

Family: Sky Beak (Father), Ocean Flow (Mother), Terramar (Brother)

Friends: Yona, Gallus, Ocellus, Smolder, Sandbar

Super excitable **Silverstream** is a Hippogriff and Seapony who is a very dedicated student at the School of Friendship.

Silverstream's mother still lives as a Seapony, but her father lives as a Hippogriff on Mount Aris.

Seaquestria

When the **Storm King** invaded the home of the Hippogriffs on Mount Aris, they fled into the sea and created a new home, called Seaquestria. **Queen Novo** rules over the kingdom and many residents share their time between here and on land, now the **Storm King** has been defeated.

The Mane Six visit Seaquestria in MY LITTLE PONY: THE MOVIE and **Queen Novo** transforms them into their Seapony forms.

Did you know?

Hippogriffia was once destroyed when the Hippogriffs fought the **Storm King's** army.

Would you like to live under the seas like Seaponies?

Ocellus

- **Species:** Changeling
- **Job:** Student at the School of Friendship
- **Lives in:** Changeling Kingdom
- **Hobbies:** Shape-shifting to make her classmates laugh
- **Dislikes:** Queen Chrysalis for giving Changelings a bad reputation and she gets scared in new situations
- **Friends:** Thorax, Pharynx, Yona, Smolder, Sandbar, Silverstream, Gallus

Ocellus is a young Changeling who loves being part of the School of Friendship. She is very shy when meeting new people and disguises herself out of her Changeling form.

Ocellus does well in **Pinkie Pie's** classes!

Changeling Kingdom

When **Queen Chrysalis** reigned over the Changeling Kingdom it was a dark place filled with hatred. Now that **Thorax** has taken over, wildlife and nature has started to return to the Kingdom.

The old Changeling hive was empty and unwelcoming.

Fun Fact!

Ocellus' home is filled with green plants and natural objects like gems and firefly night lights.

Yona

Species: Yak

Job: Student at the School of Friendship

Lives in: Yakyakistan

Hobbies: Smashing things

Dislikes: Water and spiders

Friends: Prince Rutherfood, Smolder, Ocellus, Sandbar, Silverstream, Gallus

Yona found joining the School of Friendship quite hard at first, as her classmates were not at all like Yaks. But the warm hearts of her friends helped her to feel at home and she grew to be more gentle and smash things less.

Yona writes an essay on her hero, **Rockhoof**, one of the Pillars of Equestria and how it's okay if he doesn't fit in right away.

Yakyakistan

The kingdom where Yaks live is called Yakyakistan and is a snowy region north of the Crystal Empire. Although it used to be closed off from the rest of Equestria, **Pinkie Pie**, **Prince Blueblood** and **Shining Armor** work with the Yak ruler, **Prince Rutherford** to make peace between the ponies and the Yaks.

Yona and the Yaks celebrate Snilldar Fest. They braid their hair and get to smash things!

Did you know?

Pinkie Pie is an honorary Yak because she once helped them escape from an avalanche.

137

Smolder

Species: Dragon

Job: Student at the School of Friendship

Lives in: Dragon Lands

Hobbies: Eating gems, fire-breathing, flying

Dislikes: Anycreature thinking she is cute, Sludge for lying to Spike

Friends: Ember, Spike, Yona, Sandbar, Ocellus, Silverstream, Gallus

One of the more fiesty of the **Young Six**, **Smolder** does not like to do as she's told and is often up to mischief with her friends.

Fun Fact!

Smolder secretly loves playing with dolls and cute things, but she doesn't want anycreature finding out!

Coming from the Dragon Lands, **Smolder** knows much more about moulting than **Spike** and she helps him learn to fly.

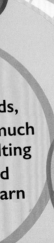

Dragon Lands

The Dragon Lands is a volcanic island which is home to Dragons and some Phoenixes. It is full of lava and rocky areas – plus gems for Dragons to eat!

Dragons do not get burned by lava, they can swim through it.

Princess Ember wins the Gauntlet of Fire contest in Dragon Lands, making her the next Dragon Lord after her father, **Torch**.

Dragon's houses are called lairs.

Sandbar

- **Species:** Earth Pony
- **Job:** Student at the School of Friendship
- **Lives in:** Ponyville
- **Hobbies:** Hanging out at Young Six's Treehouse
- **Dislikes:** Friends falling out and failing in class
- **Friends:** Yona, Gallus, Smolder, Silverstream, Ocellus
- **Cutie Mark:**

Sandbar is a student at **Twilight's** School of Friendship and a member of the **Young Six.** A laidback member of the group, **Sandbar** loves to help a friend in need and keep everycreature smiling.

Sandbar was once chased by a Bugbear after **Discord** set him on the students.

Did you know?

Sandbar pretends to betray his friends to catch out **Cozy Glow**, but in real life he is always loyal.

Treehouse

The **Young Six** hang out in a treehouse made from the roots of the Tree of Harmony.

Who's in the treehouse?

The Tree of Harmony was destroyed by **King Sombra** in Season Eight.

Cutie Mark Crusaders

The Crusaders' cutie marks all sit on the same shield background, tying them all together.

The Cutie Mark Crusaders is a club which was founded by Apple Bloom, Scootaloo and Sweetie Belle, with the aim of helping each other to discover their cutie marks. They tried everything they could think of to get their cutie marks. It wasn't until they tried to help their friend, **Gabby the Griffon,** (it didn't work because Griffon's don't get cutie marks) that they figured out their special skill was helping ponies to find their destinies.

Apple Bloom

Species: Earth Pony

Job: Tutor at the School of Friendship

Lives in: Sweet Apple Acres

Hobbies: Dancing, helping out on the farm

Dislikes: When Applejack bosses her around

Family: The Apple family

Friends: Fellow crusaders, Zecora

Cutie Mark:

Scootaloo

Species: Pegasus

Job: Tutor at the School of Friendship

Lives in: Ponyville

Hobbies: Watching the Wonderbolts and riding her scooter

Dislikes: Not being able to fly

Family: Auntie Lofty and Aunt Holiday

Friends: Fellow crusaders, Rainbow Dash

Cutie Mark:

Sweetie Belle

Species: Unicorn

Job: Tutor at the School of Friendship

Lives in: Ponyville

Hobbies: Singing, making clothes, cooking

Dislikes: Being over shadowed by her sister, Rarity.

Family: Rarity (sister), Hondo Flanks (father), Cookie Crumbles (mother)

Friends: Fellow crusaders

Cutie Mark:

The Wonderbolts

Spitfire

- **Species:** Pegasus
- **Job:** Wonderbolt (retired)
- **Lives in:** Cloudsdale
- **Hobbies:** Training, training, training.
- **Dislikes:** Losing competitions
- **Family:** The Wonderbolts are like family
- **Friends:** Rainbow Dash, Soarin and Blaze
- **Cutie Mark:**

The **Wonderbolt's** are the best fliers in all of Equestria and perform aerial acrobatics at flying competitions on Cloudsdale. The Wonderbolts are led by **Spitfire** but it's members also include **Soarin, Blaze, Fleetfoot, Rapidfire** and **Rainbow Dash!**

The Wonderbolts are always looking for new recruits. In Season Six **Sky Stinger, Vapor Trail** and **Angel Wings** join the squad.

144

The Wonderbolt Academy

The Wonderbolts train new recruits at the Wonderbolt Academy in Cloudsdale. The Academy includes a runway, obstacle course and the Dizzitron. Both **Fluttershy** and **Rainbow Dash** trained here as fillies, but it was Dash's passion for flying that got her a spot on the squad.

Spitfire used to be a drill sergeant at the Academy. She put all the new recruits through their paces!

Did you know?

The Wonderbolts were created by **General Firefly** who assembled the first aerial squadron to protect **Princess Celestia** and help keep the peace during **Princess Luna's** banishment.

The Apple Family

Braebrun

⭐ **Species:** Earth Pony

⭐ **Job:** Farmer

⭐ **Lives in:** Appleloosa

⭐ **Hobbies:** Competing in rodeos and tending to his crops

⭐ **Dislikes:** Rotten apples

⭐ **Family:** The Apple Family

⭐ **Friends:** Little Strongheart

⭐ **Cutie Mark:**

The Apple's are one of the biggest families in Equestria and **Applejack** loves to get them all together for family reunions. Applejack often spends time with her cousin, **Braeburn**, and goes to visit him in his apple orchard in Appleloosa.

Applejack helps **Braeburn** become friends with **Little Strongheart** and the Buffalo tribe when they're fighting over land in Appleloosa.

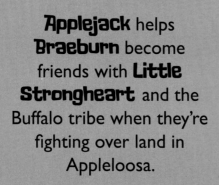

Appleloosa

Appleloosa is home to lots of Earth ponies, including many of the Apple family. The town has acres of apple orchards, a saloon called the Salt Block and a big, red clock tower.

Fun Fact!

The apple pie's made from Appleloosa's apples are so tasty that they convinced **Chief Thunderhooves** to make peace with the Appleloosans.

Can you spot the red clocktower?

Zecora

- **Species:** Zebra
- **Job:** Herbalist
- **Lives in:** Everfree Forest
- **Hobbies:** Singing
- **Dislikes:** Ponies being afraid of her
- **Friends:** The Mane Six, Apple Bloom

Zecora is Equestria's magical healer. She lives in a hut in the Everfree Forest where she makes her medicines and potions.

Did you know?

Zecora almost always talks in rhyme.

The ponies always go to **Zecora** when they need help. Zecora helped **Spike** when he started shedding his scales and helped **Rarity** regain her hearing.

Zecora's Hut

Zecora's home is made from a hollowed-out tree. The walls are circular and she collects interesting artefacts including a dream catcher and a crystal ball.

She decorates her home with masks and potion bottles.

Zecora mixes her magical potions and medicines in a large cauldron.

Pillars of Old Equestria

Long ago, a Unicorn named **Stygian** brought together six ponies to protect Equestria from evil. These six ponies became known as the **Pillars of Old Equestria.** However, the legend goes that Stygian grew jealous of the Pillars and resented their power. After stealing items from each of the Pillars, he was exiled from Equestria, which made him angry and his anger turned him into a dark force called the **Pony of Shadows.**

The only way for the **Pillars** to get rid of the Pony of Shadows was to banish it, and themselves, into limbo.

Rockhoof

Star Swirl the Bearded ● ● ● ➤

Somnambula

Mistmane

Mage Meadowbrook

Many moons later, when **Twilight Sparkle** and her friends find an old spell book and release the Pillars from their prison, they also release the **Pony of Shadows**. **Twilight Sparkle** realises that **Stygian** is in fact trapped inside the **Pony of Shadows** and he feels scared and afraid – he says he only stole the items from the **Pillars** so that he could gain some power and help them. Now, he needs the support of a friend to help him come back. Twilight convinces the **Mane Six** and the **Pillars** to help save **Stygian** and together they restore him to his pony form.

Flash Magnus

Pillar: Star Swirl the Bearded

- **Species:** Unicorn
- **Virtue:** Sorcery
- **Job:** Conjurer
- **Object Stolen:** Journal
- **Pony pairing:** Twilight
- **Lives in:** Travels all over Equestria

Star Swirl is a well-known conjuror from history and **Twilight** is his number one fan. When they first meet he is angry with her for bringing back the **Pony of Shadows**, but she teaches him that those who seem like enemies may just need the help of a friend.

In the present day, **Star Swirl** travels all over Equestria, learning about new ideas of friendship and magic. He is just as much a fan of **Twilight** as she is of him.

Pillar: Mage Meadowbrook

Mage Meadowbrook, a legendary healer whose story was told to **Fluttershy** by her parents as a filly. She is said to have studied medicine long ago and travelled around Equestria helping sick ponies. Then one day, she suddenly vanished and no one saw her again.

Species: Earth Pony

Virtue: Healing

Job: Healer

Object Stolen: Healing mask

Pony pairing: Fluttershy

Lives in: Hayseed Swamp

Fluttershy uses **Mage Meadowbrook's** remedy for swamp fever to cure **Zecora.**

Pillar: Flash Magnus

Species: Pegasus

Virtue: Bravery

Job: Drill sergeant of the Canterlot Royal Guide, star member of the Cloudsdale Royal Legion (previously)

Object Stolen: Fireproof shield

Pony pairing: Rainbow Dash

Lives in: Cloudsdale

Flash Magnus is the hero of **Rainbow Dash's** favourite campfire tale. In the story, when **Flash's** fellow soldiers are captured in a dragon's lair, he acts as bait in order for the soldiers to escape. In the present, Flash is a drill sergeant for **Princess Celestia's** guard.

His fire-proof shield, Netitus, is awarded to him by his commanding officer for bravery.

Pillar: Rockhoof

Rockhoof is said to have saved his village from a volcanic eruption by building a dam to change the route of the lava flow. His efforts transformed him from a small pony into a large and powerful stallion.

Species: Earth Pony

Virtue: Strength

Job: Keeper of Equestrian tales, Member of the Mighty Helm (previously)

Object Stolen: Shovel

Pony pairing: Applejack

Lives in: Small village at foot of a volcano

Cutie Mark:

Rockhoof has found it hard to fit into present day Equestria. He tries lots of new jobs, including becoming a teacher at the School of Friendship.

Pillar: Somnambula

Species: Pegasus

Virtue: Hope

Job: Motivational speaker, advisor to Prince Hisan (previously)

Object Stolen: Blindfold

Pony pairing: Pinkie Pie

Lives in: Somnambula

Somnambula is a brave and clever pony, who saved her village from an evil sphinx. When Prince Hisan was captured, **Somnambula** solved the sphinx's riddle and walked a tightrope blindfolded, banishing the sphinx forever. In the present day, she works as a motivational speaker.

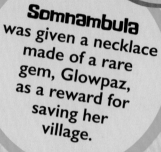

Somnambula was given a necklace made of a rare gem, Glowpaz, as a reward for saving her village.

Pillar: Mistmane

Mistmane's story is **Rarity's** favourite campfire tale. The story goes that Mistmane was a beautiful Unicorn who looked after the gardens of the Crystal Empire. But her beauty made someponies jealous and so Mistmane sacrificed her own beauty and gave it to her friends.

Species: Unicorn

Virtue: Selfless

Job: Sorceress, Crystal Empire landscaper (previously)

Object Stolen: Everlasting flower

Pony pairing: Rarity

Lives in: Crystal Empire

Cutie Mark:

Rarity is just like **Mistmane**, she would give up anything for her friends happiness.

Pony of Shadows

- **Species:** Unicorn

- **Powers:** Spreading darkness, flying

- **Nemesis:** Pillars of Old Equestria

- **Weaknesses:** Secretly cares about friendship and wants to be loved

- **Hobbies:** Trying to defeat Pillars, escape from limbo

When **Stygian** felt rejected by the **Pillars of Equestria**, his anger and jealousy took over him and he became the **Pony of Shadows**. His aim was to spread darkness over Equestria.

The **Pony of Shadows** was created from the leftover dark magic of **Nightmare Moon**, feeding on **Stygian's** anger.

Stygian

Stygian is a shy and kind pony who brought together the Pillars to protect Equestria. His anger trapped him inside the **Pony of Shadows**, but **Starlight Glimmer** and **Twilight Sparkle** helped him to see he was not a villain after all.

Species: Unicorn

Job: Author, founder of the Pillars of Old Equestria (previously)

Lives in: Hollow Shades

Hobbies: Writing, travelling Equestria

Dislikes: Letting anypony down, feeling left out

Friends: Star Swirl the Bearded, Starlight Glimmer

Star Swirl apologises to **Stygian** because he mistakenly thought he was trying to steal the **Pillars'** power.

Meet the Villains

Storm King

Tempest Shadow

Lord Tirek

Lord Tirek

Species: Centaur

Powers: Super strength, magic absorbing, shoots beams from horns

Nemesis: Twilight Sparkle

Weaknesses: Underestimates ponies' magic

Hobbies: Stealing ponies magic, lying and scheming

Tirek is still a power-hungry centaur who dreams of ruling over Equestria. He steals magic from everypony and tricks creatures into helping him.

Many years ago, **Tirek** and his brother, **Scorpan**, travelled to Equestria to defeat the ponies and take over the kingdom. But when Scorpan arrived and got to know someponies, he changed his mind and begged Tirek to stop. Tirek was determined to gain control, so Scorpan told the Princesses of his brother's evil plans and they imprisioned Tirek in Tartarus, Equestria's prison.

Tirek was given a medallion by his brother, **Scorpan**. The medallion turned out to be the final key needed to unlock the Tree of Harmony's chest in **Twilight's** Kingdom. It gave the **Mane Six** the power to overthrow **Tirek** and return him to prison.

Evil fact:

The more magic **Tirek** steals, the larger he becomes. When he steals the magic of many ponies, he gets bigger, turns bright red and grows horns.

Did you know?

Tirek is responsible for destroying **Twilight's** Golden Oak Library.

163

Chrysalis

Species: Changeling

Powers: Shape-shifting, magic absorbing, telekinesis (moving things with her mind), extreme intelligence, great strength

Nemesis: Starlight Glimmer

Weaknesses: Boastful about her power (which can leave her distracted) and poor acting skills (she sometimes gives herself away when shape-shifting)

Hobbies: Creating terror in ponies, plotting more evil plans and feeding off otherponies' love

No matter how many times she's defeated, **Chrysalis** always seems to return. In Season Nine, she teams up with **Tirek** and **Cozy Glow** to defeat the **Mane Six** and **Starlight Glimmer** once and for all.

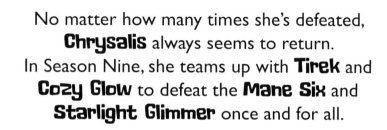

Evil fact:

Chrysalis is the first major villain to have her own song.

In Season Two, **Chrysalis** captured and impersonated **Princess Cadance** to feed off **Prince Shining Armor's** love for his bride.

Chrysalis can **shape-shift** to disguise herself. She can look like any other pony or creature, so you never know where she might be lurking!

Top disguises:

Mean Applejack

Photographer

Mean Rarity

King Sombra

- ★ **Species:** Unicorn
- ★ **Powers:** Moves in shadow form, stops Unicorn's magic, hypnosis
- ★ **Nemesis:** Crystal ponies
- ★ **Weaknesses:** Underestimates the value of teamwork
- ★ **Hobbies:** Plotting to capture the Crystal Heart

Sombra wears strong armour to protect him.

King Sombra is a power-hungry Unicorn who once ruled over the Crystal Empire and enslaved the Crystal ponies. Using the magic of the Crystal Heart, the Princesses manage to banish Sombra. But determined to come back, Sombra hypnotises the ponies of Canterlot and almost takes over Equestria until the Mane Six intervene.

Sombra steals baby Flurry Heart in the Crystal Empire.

Evil fact:

King Sombra prefers to work alone and won't work with Grogar's ultimate evil team.

Cozy Glow

- **Species:** Pegasus
- **Powers:** Cunning, plotting, tricking other ponies
- **Nemesis:** The Young Six
- **Weaknesses:** No real magic so can be easily defeated if her plans do not work
- **Hobbies:** Making friends with ponies in order to use them later

Cozy Glow makes friends with **Tirek** and works with **Grogar** to come up with a new plan to take over Equestria.

Evil fact:

Cosy Glow is the youngest villian to ever take on the **Mane Six.**

Sweet **Cozy Glow** is a mastermind at plotting. She tricked the **Crusaders** and made friends with **Twilight Sparkle**, so that she could take over the School of Friendship. She even captured the magic of the Elements of Harmony so that she could be the Empress of Friendship. The **Young Six**, **Mane Six** and princesses worked together to defeat the evil Pegasus and trap her in Tartarus.

Chancellor Neighsay almost ruins Cozy's plan when he takes over the School of Friendship.

Did you know?

Cozy Glow makes **Tirek** a best friend sculpture.

Grogar

Species: Unknown Creature

Powers: Magic, manipulation

Nemesis: Twilight Sparkle

Weaknesses: Can't convince all the villians to work together

Hobbies: Making evil plans, taking down Twilight Sparkle

Evil fact:

Grogar is an ancient villain who appears in stories with **Gutsy the Great.** Most ponies don't believe he's real, but he attempts to take over Equestria in Season Nine.

When **Princess Celestia** and **Princess Luna** ask **Twilight Sparkle** and her friends to take over ruling Equestria, they're very nervous. But soon they have an even bigger probem when the most fearsome villian of all time, the legendary **Grogar**, unites their past enemies **Chrysalis, Tirek, Cozy Glow** and **King Sombra** to take over Equestria once and for all.

Discord is struck down by **King Sombra's** magic when he takes over the Crystal Empire.

King Sombra refuses to follow **Grogar's** plans and tries to defeat the ponies by himself.

Storm King

- ⭐ **Species:** Unknown Creature

- ⭐ **Powers:** Controls the Staff of Sacanas, giving him the power to drain Alicorn magic

- ⭐ **Nemesis:** Twilight Sparkle

- ⭐ **Weaknesses:** He breaks his promise to Tempest, causing her to desert him

- ⭐ **Hobbies:** Turning things to stone, plotting evil plans

The **Storm King** dreams of taking over Equestria and beyond. He fought the Hippogriffs, destroying their home and forcing them to live in Sequestria as Seaponies. In *MY LITTLE PONY: THE MOVIE*, he tries to take the magic of the four princesses, but he is defeated by **Tempest Shadow** and the **Mane Six.**

The **Storm King** uses the staff to create a powerful tornado which stops **Twilight** from using her magic.

172

Tempest Shadow

When we first meet **Tempest Shadow,** she is helping the **Storm King** in his quest to rule Equestria. But when she discovers that the **Storm King** won't restore her horn, she decides to help **Twilight** defeat him.

Species: Unicorn

Powers: Super-strength, firework displays

Nemesis: The Storm King

Hobbies: Writing, travelling Equestria

Weaknesses: She feels self conscious about her broken horn, which leads her to make bad choices

Hobbies: Travelling Equestria

Evil fact:

Tempest has a trusty sidekick, **Grubber.**

Tartarus

Tartarus is a dark and scary place. Only the most evil villains are sent there.

Did you know?

Tirek is the only villain to have ever escaped Tartarus by himself. Thanks to **Discord's** help, he escapes again with **Cozy Glow**.

In Season Two, **Cozy Glow** is sent to Tartarus for taking over the School of Friendship when she tried to become Empress of Friendship.

Tartarus is where all the ancient, evil creatures are imprisoned. **Lord Tirek** escapes from Tartarus and takes over Equestria in his pursuit of everypony's magic. He imprisons **Princesses Celestia, Luna** and **Cadance** there as revenge for his own imprisonment. Luckily **Princess Twilight** and her friends save the princesses and return **Tirek** to the prison.

Tartarus is guarded by a three-headed dog.

Cutie Map

Fun Fact!

The Cutie Map first appears in Season Five.

When the map summons one of the friends, their cutie marks glow and pulsate.

After the Cutie Map appeared in **Twilight's** Castle of Friendship, the **Mane Six** and their friends began to be summoned across Equestria on Friendship quests. On these quests the ponies meet all sorts of creatures who need help solving a friendship problem.

The ponies cutie marks appear on the map where their friendship lessons are needed.

Come and meet everycreature!

Meet the Characters

Coriander Cumin

Species: Unicorn

Lives in: Canterlot

Job: Restaurant owner

Hobbies: Cooking

Family: Saffron Masala (Daughter)

Cutie Mark:

Saffron Massala

Species: Unicorn

Lives in: Canterlot

Job: Chef at Tasty Treat restaurant

Hobbies: Trying new recipes

Family: Coriander Cumin (Father)

Cutie Mark:

Alice

Species: Reindeer

Lives in: Arctic North

Job: Gift Giver at the Grove

Friends: Pinkie Pie, Aurora and Bori (Gift Givers)

Bori

Species: Reindeer

Lives in: Arctic North

Job: Gift Giver at the Grove

Hobbies: Helping ponies find the perfect gift

Friends: Pinkie Pie, Aurora and Alice (Gift Givers)

Aurora

Species: Reindeer

Lives in: Arctic North

Job: Gift Giver at the Grove

Hobbies: Helping ponies find the perfect gift

Friend: Pinkie Pie, Alice and Bori (Gift Givers)

Sunny Skies

Species: Unicorn

Lives in: Hope Hollow

Job: Mayor of Hope Hollow

Hobbies: Spending time with Petunia

Friend: Petunia Petals

Cutie Mark:

Fancy Pants

Species: Unicorn

Lives in: Canterlot

Job: Celebrity

Hobbies: Attending parties

Friend: Fleur de Lis

Cutie Mark:

Hoity Toity

Species: Earth

Lives in: Canterlot

Job: Fashion critic

Hobbies: Attending fashion shows

Friend: Rarity

Cutie Mark:

Meet the Characters

Big McIntosh

Species: Earth

Lives in: Sweet Apple Acres

Job: Farmer, Pony Tones singer

Hobbies: Helping Sugar Belle

Family: Apple family, Sugar Belle (Girlfriend)

Cutie Mark:

Granny Smith

Species: Earth

Lives in: Sweet Apple Acres

Job: Apple farmer

Hobbies: Hosting Apple family reunions

Family: Apple family

Cutie Mark:

Sugar Belle

Species: Unicorn

Lives in: Our town

Job: Baker

Hobbies: Baking

Friend: Big Mac (Boyfriend)

Cutie Mark:

Auntie Applesauce

Species: Earth

Lives in: Ponyville

Job: Jam maker (retired)

Hobbies: Partying in Las Pegasus

Family: Applejack

Cutie Mark:

Apple Rose

Species: Earth

Lives in: Appleloosa

Job: Retired

Hobbies: Visiting Las Pegasus

Family: Granny Smith's favourite cousin

Babs Seed

Species: Earth

Lives in: Manehatten

Job: Student

Hobbies: Leading the Manehatten Cutie Mark Crusaders

Friends: The Apple Family

Cherry Jubilee

Species: Earth

Lives in: Dodge Junction

Job: Owner of Cherry Hill Ranch

Hobbies: Going to rodeos

Friend: Applejack

Cutie Mark:

Petunia Petals

Species: Earth

Lives in: Hope Hollow

Job: Running the hotel/library/ visitor centre

Hobbies: Reading, helping the town

Friend: Mayor Sunny Skies

Cutie Mark:

Meet the Characters

Night Light

Species: Unicorn

Lives in: Canterlot

Hobbies: Playing bingo

Family: Twilight Sparkle (daughter), Shining Armor (son), Twilight Velvet (wife)

Cutie Mark:

Princess Flurry Heart

Species: Alicorn

Lives in: Crystal Empire

Family: Princess Cadance (mother), Shining Armor (father), Night Light (grandfather), Twilight Velvet (grandmother), Twilight Sparkle (aunt)

Prince Blueblood

Species: Unicorn

Lives in: Canterlot

Job: Far too royal to work

Hobbies: Being groomed

Friends: Princess Celestia, Princess Luna, Princess Cadance

Cutie Mark:

Prince Shining Armor

Species: Unicorn

Lives in: Crystal Empire

Job: Co-ruler of the Crystal Empire, Captain of the Canterlot Royal Guard

Family: Princess Cadance (wife), Flurry Heart (daughter)

Cutie Mark:

Twilight Velvet

Species: Unicorn

Lives in: Canterlot

Hobbies: Bungee jumping

Family: Twilight Sparkle (daughter), Shining Armor (son), Night Light (husband)

Cutie Mark:

Sassy Saddles

Species: Unicorn

Lives in: Canterlot, Trottingham (previously)

Job: Manager of Canterlot Carousel

Hobbies: Fashion

Friend: Rarity

Twinkleshine

Species: Unicorn

Lives in: Canterlot

Job: Ponyville choir member

Hobbies: Singing, partying

Friends: Lemon Hearts, Minuette, Moon Dancer

Cutie Mark:

Upper Crust

Species: Unicorn

Lives in: Canterlot

Hobbies: Attending upper class events

Family: Jet Set (husband)

Friend: Fancy Pants

Meet the Characters

Thorax

Species: Changeling

Lives in: Changeling Kingdom

Job: Leader of the Changelings

Hobbies: Making friends

Family: Pharynx

Pharynx

Species: Changeling

Lives in: Changeling Kingdom

Job: Head of patrol

Hobbies: Protecting the hive, looking after his brother

Family: Thorax (brother)

Windy Whistles

Species: Pegasus

Lives in: Cloudsdale

Job: Proud mum

Hobbies: Supporting Dash

Family: Rainbow Dash (daughter), Bow Hothoof (husband)

Cutie Mark:

Bow Hothoof

Species: Pegasus

Lives in: Cloudsdale

Job: Proud dad

Hobbies: Supporting Dash in her competitions

Family: Rainbow Dash (daughter), Windy Whistles (wife)

Cutie Mark:

Flitter

Species: Pegasus

Lives in: Cloudsdale

Job: Weather controller

Hobbies: Flying races

Friend: Cloudchaser

Cutie Mark:

Lightning Dust

Species: Pegasus

Lives in: Cloudsdale

Job: Leader of the Washouts, a rival group to the Wonderbolts

Nemesis: Rainbow Dash

Cutie Mark:

Mr Shy

Species: Pegasus

Lives in: Cloudsdale

Job: Retired weather controller

Hobbies: Cloud collecting

Family: Fluttershy (daughter), Mrs Shy (wife), Zephyr Breeze (son)

Cutie Mark:

Zephyr Breeze

Species: Pegasus

Lives in: Cloudsdale

Job: Mane therapist

Hobbies: Lots of different things, Zephyr struggles to stick to anything!

Family: Fluttershy (sister)

Cutie Mark:

Meet the Characters

Soarin

Species: Pegasus

Lives in: Cloudsdale

Job: Wonderbolt

Hobbies: Eating apple pies!

Friends: The Wonderbolts

Cutie Mark:

Wind Rider

Species: Pegasus

Lives in: Cloudsdale

Job: Wonderbolt (retired)

Hobbies: Flying Mustang Marathons

Cutie Mark:

Chancellor Neighsay

Species: Unicorn

Lives in: Canterlot

Job: Head of Equestria Education Association

Hobbies: Keeping order

Nemesis: Twilight Sparkle

Rolling Thunder

Species: Pegasus

Lives in: Cloudsdale

Job: Member of the Washouts

Hobbies: Flying, stunts

Friends: Short Fuse, Lightning Dust

Bulk Biceps

Species: Pegasus

Lives in: Cloudsdale

Job: Wonderbolt trainee, weightlifter

Hobbies: Working out

Cutie Mark:

Clear Skies

Species: Pegasus

Lives in: Cloudsdale

Job: Weather controller

Hobbies: Clearing the weather

Friends: Sunshower, Open Skies

Cutie Mark:

Tank

Species: Tortoise

Lives in: Cloudsdale

Job: Rainbow Dash's pet

Hobbies: Flying

Friends: Rainbow Dash, Fluttershy, Pinkie Pie

Tight Ship

Species: Pegasus

Lives in: Cloudsdale

Job: Training Wonderbolts cadets

Hobbies: Planning training schedules

Friends: The Wonderbolts

Meet the Characters

Amethyst Maresbury

Species: Earth

Lives in: Crystal Empire

Job: Librarian

Hobbies: Reading

Friend: Sunburst

Cutie Mark:

Blaze

Species: Pegasus

Lives in: Crystal Empire

Job: Wonderbolt

Hobbies: Science experiments

Friends: Surprise, Soarin'

Cutie Mark:

Chief Thunderhooves

Species: Buffalo

Lives in: Tribe near Appleloosa

Job: Chief of the Buffalo tribe

Hobbies: Stampeding along trails

Friends: Little Strongheart

Sunburst

Species: Unicorn

Lives in: Crystal Empire

Job: Flurry Heart's Crystaller

Hobbies: Reading

Family & Friends: Stella Flare (Mother), Starlight Glimmer and Trixie

Cutie Mark:

Torque Wrench

Species: Earth

Lives in: Hope Hollow

Job: Handi-pony

Hobbies: Fixing broken things

Friend: Mayor Sunny Skies

Cutie Mark:

Gladmane

Species: Earth

Lives in: Las Pegasus

Job: Business owner (retired)

Friends: Flim and Flam

Princess Ember

Species: Dragon

Lives in: Dragon Lands

Job: Dragon Lord

Hobbies: Lava surfing

Friends: Spike, Thorax

Angel Bunny

Species: Rabbit

Lives in: Everfree Forest

Job: Fluttershy's pet

Hobbies: Bossing other animals around

Friend: Fluttershy

Meet the Characters

Daring Do

Species: Pegasus

Lives in: Forest north-west of the Galloping Gorge and north-east of Vanhoover Treasure hunter

Job: Writing adventure stories

Family: Gallant True (uncle)

Cutie Mark:

AK Yearling

Species: Pegasus

Lives in: Galloping Gorge

Job: Novelist, Treasure Hunter

Hobbies: Defeating baddies

Friend: Rainbow Dash

Gabby

Species: Griffon

Lives in: Griffonstone

Job: Mail courier

Hobbies: Member of Cutie Mark Crusaders

Friends: Scootaloo, Sugarbelle, Apple Bloom

Gilda

Species: Griffon

Lives in: Griffonstone

Job: Scone baker

Hobbies: Flying super fast

Friend: Rainbow Dash

Autumn Blaze

Species: Kirin

Lives in: Kirin Village

Job: Cures the silence spell affecting the Kirins

Hobbies: Singing

Friend: Rain Shine (leader of Kirin village)

Capper

Species: Cat

Lives in: Klugetown

Job: Con artist

Hobbies: Tricking ponies

Friend: Rarity

Flim

Species: Unicorn

Lives in: Las Pegasus

Job: Travelling salesponies and Las Pegasus resort owner

Hobbies: Money-making deals

Family: Flam (brother)

Cutie Mark:

Flam

Species: Unicorn

Lives in: Las Pegasus

Job: Travelling salesponies and Las Pegasus resort owner

Hobbies: Money-making deals

Family: Flim (brother)

Cutie Mark:

Meet the Characters

Sapphire Shores

Species: Earth

Lives in: Canterlot

Job: Pop star

Hobbies: Singing, going to fashion shows

Friend: Hoity Toity

Dj Pon-3

Species: Unicorn

Lives in: Manehattan

Job: Disc jockey

Hobbies: Listening to hip-hop music

Friend: 33⅓-LP

Cutie Mark:

Dr Cabelleron

Species: Earth

Lives in: Manehattan

Job: Archaeologist

Hobbies: Stealing artifacts

Friends: Ahuizotl (partner in crime), Henchponies

Cutie Mark:

Mr Stripes

Species: Earth

Lives in: Manehattan

Job: Landlord

Hobbies: Supporting his daughter's unusual ideas

Family: Plaid Stripes (daughter)

Cutie Mark:

Opalescense

Species: Persian cat

Lives in: Manehattan

Job: Rarity's pet

Hobbies: Hanging out with Rarity

Friends: Rarity

Cheese Sandwich

Species: Earth

Lives in: Manehattan

Job: Party planner

Hobbies: Playing the accordian, singing

Friend: Pinkie Pie

Cutie Mark:

Coloratura

Species: Earth

Lives in: Manehattan

Job: Pop star

Hobbies: Singing, doing charity work, meeting young foals

Friend: Applejack

Cutie Mark:

Miss Pommel

Species: Earth

Lives in: Manehattan

Job: Bridleway dressmaker

Hobbies: Performing in the Midsummer Theatre Revival

Friend: Rarity

Cutie Mark:

Meet the Characters

Terramar

Species: Hippogriff

Lives in: Mount Aris and Seaquestria

Job: Student at the School of Friendship

Hobbies: Eating kelp crisps

Family: Sky Beak (father), Silverstream (sister), Ocean Flow (mother)

Sky Beak

Species: Hippogriff

Lives in: Mount Aris

Job: Royal duties

Hobbies: Playing festival games

Family: Terramar (son), Silverstream (daughter), Queen Novo (sister) Ocean Flow (wife)

Princess Skystar

Species: Seapony

Lives in: Seaquestria

Job: Princess of Equestria

Hobbies: Avoiding school with her friends

Family: Queen Novo (mother), Silverstream, Terramar (cousins)

Queen Novo

Species: Seapony

Lives in: Seaquestria

Job: Ruler of Seaquestria

Hobbies: Having a seaweed wrap and massage

Family: Sky Beak (brother-in-law), Princess Skystar (daughter), Ocean Flow (sister)

Ocean Flow

Species: Seapony

Lives in: Seaquestria

Hobbies: Picnics on the beach

Family: Sky Beak (husband) Silverstream (daughter) Terramar (son)

Prince Rutherford

Species: Yak

Lives in: Yakyakistan

Job: Ruler of Yaks

Hobbies: Stomping and smashing things

Friends: Yona, Pinkie Pie

Hondo Flanks

Species: Unicorn

Lives in: Ponyville

Hobbies: Giving cart rides to friends and fishing

Family: Rarity (daughter), Cookie Crumbles (wife), Sweetie Belle (daughter)

Cutie Mark:

Cookie Crumbles

Species: Unicorn

Lives in: Ponyville

Job: Teaching Sweetie Belle to cook

Family: Hondo Flanks (husband), Rarity, Sweetie Belle (daughters)

Cutie Mark:

Meet the Characters

Marble Pie

Species: Earth

Lives in: Pie Family Rock Farm, Rockville

Family: Limestone, Maud, Pinkie, (sisters) Igneous Rock Pie (father), Cloudy Quartz (mother), Feldspar Granite Pie (grandfather)

Cutie Mark:

Cloudy Quartz

Species: Earth

Lives in: Pie Family Rock Farm, Rockville

Job: Rock Farmer

Family: Marble, Limestone, Maud, Pinkie, (daughters) Igneous Rock Pie (husband)

Cutie Mark:

Igneous Rock Pie

Species: Earth

Lives in: Pie Family Rock Farm, Rockville

Job: Rock Farmer

Family: Marble, Limestone, Maud, Pinkie, (daughters), Cloudy Quartz (wife), Feldspar Granite Pie (father)

Cutie Mark:

Limestone Pie

Species: Earth

Lives in: Pie Family Rock Farm, Rockville

Family: Marble, Maud, Pinkie, (sisters) Igneous Rock Pie (father), Cloudy Quartz (mother), Feldspar Granite Pie (grandfather)

Cutie Mark:

Maud Pie

Species: Earth

Lives in: Ponyville, crystal cave

Job: Geologist, Stand-up Comic

Family: Limestone, Marble, Pinkie, (sisters) Igneous Rock Pie (father), Cloudy Quartz (mother), Feldspar Granite Pie (grandfather)

Cranky Doodle

Species: Donkey

Lives in: Ponyville

Job: Substitute Teacher at the School of Friendship

Hobbies: Being Grumpy

Family: Matilda (wife)

Diamond Tiara

Species: Earth

Lives in: Ponyville

Job: Cutie Mark Crusader student

Hobbies: Baking pies

Family: Filthy Rich (father) Spoiled Rich (mother)

Cutie Mark:

Filthy Rich

Species: Earth

Lives in: Ponyville

Job: Businesspony and Mayor of Ponyville

Hobbies: Charitable giving

Family: Spoiled Rich (wife) Diamond Tiara (daughter)

Cutie Mark:

Meet the Characters

Dr Hooves

Species: Earth

Lives in: Ponyville

Job: Time-keeper

Hobbies: Fashion, judging competitions

Friend: Derpy

Cutie Mark:

Dr Horse

Species: Earth

Lives in: Ponyville

Job: Pony doctor

Hobbies: Watching sports events

Friend: Nurse Snowheart

Cutie Mark:

Featherweight

Species: Pegasus

Lives in: Ponyville

Job: Student

Hobbies: Editor-in-Chief of school magazine, Foal Free Press

Friends: Cutie Mark Crusaders

Scorpion

Species: Gargoyle

Lives in: A distant land

Job: A reformed thief

Hobbies: Spreading the ponies way of friendship

Family: Lord Tirek (brother), King Vorak (father), Queen Haydon (mother)

Gummy

Species: Alligator

Lives in: Ponyville

Job: Pinkie Pie's pet

Hobbies: Biting, dancing

Friend: Pinkie Pie

Iron Will

Species: Minotaur

Lives in: Ponyville

Job: Self help guru, cruise director

Hobbies: Shouting at everypony

Friend: Fluttershy

Lily Valley

Species: Earth

Lives in: Ponyville

Job: Florist

Hobbies: Gardening

Friends: Daisy, Rose

Cutie Mark:

Mayor Mare

Species: Earth

Lives in: Ponyville

Job: Mayor of Ponyville

Hobbies: Presiding over town events

Friend: Pinkie Pie

Cutie Mark:

Meet the Characters

Pipsqueak

Species: Earth

Lives in: Ponyville

Job: Ponyville schoolhouse class president

Hobbies: Camping, flying his kite

Friends: Cutie Mark Crusaders, Diamond Tiara

Silver Spoon

Species: Earth

Lives in: Ponyville

Job: Student

Hobbies: Throwing parties

Friend: Diamond Tiara

Cutie Mark:

Starstreak

Species: Earth

Lives in: Ponyville

Job: Fashion designer, Avant-garde style

Hobbies: Making clothes

Friends: Inky Rose, Lily Lace

Cutie Mark:

Twist

Species: Earth

Lives in: Ponyville

Job: Student

Hobbies: Baking, making sweets

Friends: Cutie Mark Crusaders

Cutie Mark:

Carrot Cake

Species: Earth

Lives in: Ponyville

Job: Confectioner and baker

Hobbies: Competing in baking competitions

Family: Cup Cake (wife), Pumpkin and Pound (his twins)

Cutie Mark:

Cup Cake

Species: Earth

Lives in: Ponyville

Job: Confectioner and baker

Hobbies: Baking!

Family: Carrot Cake (husband), Pumpkin and Pound (her twins)

Cutie Mark:

Lyra Heartstrings

Species: Unicorn

Lives in: Ponyville

Job: Member of Ponyville Choir

Hobbies: Singing

Friend: Bon Bon

Cutie Mark:

Zipporwhill

Species: Pegasus

Lives in: Ponyville

Job: Student

Hobbies: Hanging out with her dog, Ripley

Family: Nightjar (father)

Cutie Mark:

Meet the Characters

Owlowiscious

Species: Owl

Lives in: Ponyville

Job: Twilight's night study buddy

Friend: Twilight Sparkle

Professor Fossil

Species: Earth

Lives in: Ponyville

Job: Archaeologist

Hobbies: Digging for fossils

Friend: Rockhoof

Cutie Mark:

Tree Hugger

Species: Earth

Lives in: Ponyville

Job: Art teacher

Hobbies: Member of the Equestrian Society for the Preservation of Rare Creatures

Friends: Fluttershy

Cutie Mark:

Lotus Blossom

Species: Earth

Lives in: Ponyville

Job: Owner of Ponyville Day Spa

Hobbies: Listening to music

Friends: Aloe

Cutie Mark:

Nurse Redheart

Species: Earth

Lives in: Ponyville

Job: Nurse at Ponyville Hospital

Friend: Nurse Tenderheart

Cutie Mark:

Mane-iac

Species: Earth

Lives in: Maretropolis

Job: Power Ponies villain

Hobbies: Using her Hairspray Ray of Doom

Nemesis: The Mane Six

Haakim

Species: Earth

Lives in: Saddle Arabia

Job: Member of Royal family

Hobbies: Visting other lands, representing Saddle Arabia

Friend: Amira

Captain Celaeno

Species: Bird

Lives in: Sea of Clouds

Job: Captain of the airship

Hobbies: Helping the Mane Six escape the Storm King

Friends: Pirates

Meet the Characters

Octavia Melody

Species: Earth

Lives in: Ponyville

Job: Cellist

Hobbies: Judging music competitions

Friend: DJ Pon-3

Cutie Mark:

Cheerliee

Species: Earth

Lives in: Ponyville

Job: Teacher

Hobbies: Going to Pony Tones concerts

Friend: Big Mac

Cutie Mark:

Dr Fauna

Species: Earth

Lives in: Ponyville

Job: Vet

Hobbies: Caring for sick animals

Friends: Fluttershy

Cutie Mark:

Firelight

Species: Unicorn

Lives in: Sire's Hollow

Job: Head of the Sire's Hollow Preservation Society

Family: Starlight Glimmer (father)

Cutie Mark:

Stellar Flare

Species: Unicorn

Lives in: Sire's Hollow

Job: Head of Sire's Hollow Development Committee

Hobbies: Helping Sunburst with his friendship mission

Family: Sunburst (son)

Cutie Mark:

Vapor Trail

Species: Pegasus

Lives in: Stratusburg

Job: Wonderbolt cade

Hobbies: Sky Stinger

Friend: Top Bolt

Cutie Mark:

Pistachio

Species: Earth

Lives in: Sweet Acorn Orchard

Job: Designer

Friends and Family: Rarity (Idol) Oak Nut (Father) Butternut (Mother)

Cutie Mark:

Winona

Species: Collie

Lives in: Sweet Apple Acres

Job: Applejack's pet

Hobbies: Helping on the farm

Friend: Applejack

Where is Tank?

Rainbow Dash's loyal pet, Tank has been hiding in this book.
Did you spot him?

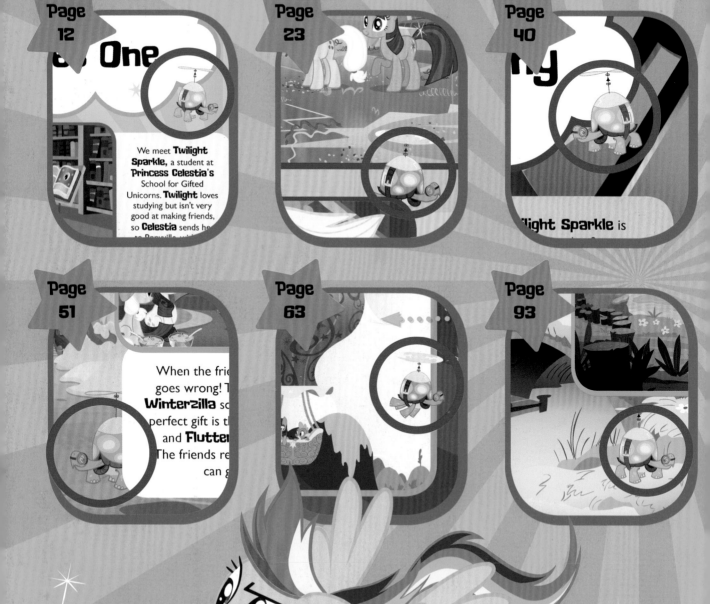

Page 12

One

We meet **Twilight Sparkle**, a student at **Princess Celestia's** School for Gifted Unicorns. **Twilight** loves studying but isn't very good at making friends, so **Celestia** sends he...

Page 23

Page 40

...light Sparkle is

Page 51

When the frie... goes wrong! T... **Winterzilla** s... perfect gift is t... and **Flutter**... The friends re... can g...

Page 63

Page 93

206

Page 100

Page 109

All kinds of exciting events happen on the farm, including Helping Hooves music festival.

Did you know?

It's

Page 126

Scho
Frien

Fun Fact!

Page 155

uof

ies: Earth Pony

ue: Strength

Keeper of Equestrian
ember of the Mighty
ously)

Page 161

Page 181

Babs Seed

ecies: Earth

es in: Manehatten

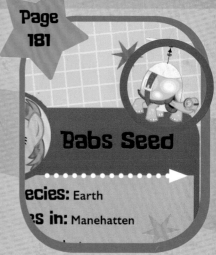

Goodbye, Everypony!

Thank you for coming on this magical adventure around Equestria with us and meeting all the Ponies, Unicorns, Yaks, Dragons, Griffons and many more creatures who live here!

We've loved sharing all the secrets of Equestria with you and helping you to get to know our friends better.

Come and visit again soon!

Love your Pony Pals,

Twilight Sparkle, Pinkie Pie, Rarity, Rainbow Dash, Fluttershy and Applejack x